A QUEST FOR JUSTICE

Also by
Frank F. Fiore

Cyberkill
The Oracle
Murran

The Chronicles of Jeremy Nash
A Taste of the Apocalypse
Seed
Black Sun

I j i n

Volume 3

A QUEST FOR JUSTICE

a novel

FRANK F. FIORE

WordCrafts

A Quest for Justice
Copyright © 2019
Frank F. Fiore

ISBN: 978-1-962218-54-2

Cover concept and design by Mike Parker.

The Ijin Trilogy was originally published in a single volume under the title of *Ijin: A Quest for Justice*.

Published by WordCrafts Press
Cody, Wyoming 82414
www.wordcrafts.net

To the American and Japanese soldiers
who gave their lives in World War Two

— THE BEGINNING OF THE END —

1944

Warrior Monk

"Where exactly are we?" Connor asked Aiko.

The train ride to the Namba Nankai station in Osaka, south of Tokyo had been long. From there they rode the express train on the Mount Koya Rail Line, then took the Mount Koya cable car to the top of the mountain.

"Mount Koya. Near the Shojoshin-in temple," she replied. "A very holy place and the home of Buddhist monks that dates back over a thousand years."

White clouds appeared below them as the cable car rumbled up the face of the mountain. Connor stared into the valley below and watched as the clouds began their habitual, silent advance up the slopes as if racing after them.

Upon arriving at the summit, he found himself standing on a mountaintop swathed in a cool breeze and surrounded by towering trees covered in a misty haze. Before them stood one of several ornate Japanese shrines.

At the end of a long, stone path, a cedar forest lined with elaborate lanterns beckoned them to enter. They stepped into the Shojoshin-in temple and were greeted by a diminutive, bald, Buddhist monk. "May I help you?" he asked respectfully.

Aiko bowed. "We're here to see Admiral Nakamura."

Connor was surprised at the request. "We're here to see an admiral?"

"A warrior monk."

"A warrior monk?" Connor repeated, confused.

Aiko placed her fingers to his lips to quiet him as the monk stretched out an arm from his black and white *kesa* robe as a sign to follow him. Connor and Aiko trailed after the man, walking through wooded aisles of a small residential area the temple. The architecture was both exquisite and ancient, making Connor feel as if he was entering a very precious place.

"Please wait here," the little monk instructed, pointing to a sitting area in a small garden of carefully arranged rocks, water falls, moss, pruned trees, and bushes. All around them, the gravel had been raked to represent ripples in water.

"It's a Zen garden," Aiko whispered. "It is intended to imitate the intimate essence of nature and to serve as an aid to meditation about the true meaning of life."

As they both sat enjoying the silence of the garden, they heard footsteps come up from behind them. They turned to see a tall, elderly Nipponese man approach. Connor guessed he must be eighty years old—perhaps older. Yet, there was an inner and outer strength to him that defied his age. He walked in an odd combination of military and contemplative style and appeared both intimidating and accessible at the same time.

Aiko stood and bowed deeply. "Nakamura-san. I would like to introduce you to my dear friend, Connor Fujiyama."

As Connor rose and bowed, Nakamura gave the boy a probing look. "Fujiyama? An American with a Japanese last name."

Aiko proceed to explain how Connor was adopted by the Fujiyamas.

"Did you say Akihito Fujiyama?"

Aiko nodded.

Nakamura finally turned his attention to Connor. "You must be very proud. Akihito Fujiyama served under my command in the Great War. He was not only an outstanding fighter pilot in my Navy, but a man with great honor."

Connor didn't respond, and Nakamura sensed much tension and conflict in the boy.

"Connor is staying with us in Tokyo for a while," Aiko interjected to break the awkward silence. "I've been showing him the better parts of Japan, the customary Japan, and I felt it would be a good idea for you to show him what I cannot."

Nakamura studied Connor and gave the boy a look that went well past his outer appearance and deep into his soul. "I see. Let us go to my quarters."

Nakamura led Connor and Aiko to his residence. They followed their host to a room with Japanese *fusuma*—sliding paper doors. Depictions of trees, animals, mountains, and villagers adorned the fusuma with great care and purpose.

An alcove in the corner of the room—a *tokonoma*—was half the size of a tatami mat and a step higher than the rest of the room, and had a small table in the center. *Kakejiku*—or hanging scrolls—*ikebana* flower arrangements, and other simple, hand carved artifacts surrounded the residence.

Everything complemented each other and made Connor feel as if he stepped into an ancient and holy place.

"I'll make some tea," Nakamura said and disappeared from the small room.

As they waited, Connor continued to survey the room, admiring elegant pieces of art and paintings, until his eyes stopped on a low table in the back of the room with a Samurai sword positioned in the center.

Connor walked up to the sword and noticed something very familiar about the ancient weapon. He looked closer. He'd seen this sword before in the painting at Fujiyama's home.

He turned to Aiko with wide eyes. "This is a famous Samurai sword. I can't remember the name of it, but it's legendary. What is the Admiral doing with it?"

"That katana," Nakamura said as he reentered the room carrying a tray of tea, "is called the *Honjo Masamune*."

Connor couldn't restrain his sheer astonishment. "You *own* the Honjo Masamune?"

Nakamura shook his head. "No. No one owns the Honjo Masamune. I am merely the custodian of the sword. That honor was bestowed upon me by Emperor Taisho, Hirohito's father."

"Why?" Connor and Aiko asked in perfect unison.

"For my naval and advisory service to Emperor Taisho."

"Then you are a *real* Samurai?" Connor blurted.

"Hai. But, unfortunately, the last of them." He placed the tea tray on the small table and began to serve his guests. "I was a man of your age, Connor-san, when I became a Samurai. Very unusual for someone of that young an age, I might add. When the Samurai fought and lost their last battle of the Satsuma Rebellion at the hands of the Imperial Army, the traditional Samurai were disbanded."

Nakamura swirled his tea. "Though the traditional Samurai were gone forever, the Emperor at the time, Emperor Mutsuhito, still wanted their counsel. I was one of the fortunate few that advised the Emperor. Then, when war with Russia came about, I joined the navy."

"And that's when you became an Admiral," Connor stated flatly.

Nakamura smiled. "Eventually."

"But—how does a military man become a monk?" Connor asked. "A *warrior* monk? That's quite a contradiction."

Nakamura took a sip of his tea. "Not really. You see, a Samurai is a spiritual person at his very core. His spirituality is just as important as his combat ability. The meditations and contemplations of Zen give the Samurai the mental discipline he needs to succeed as a warrior. This mental discipline was popular with Samurai, who understood the need to train and practice until their combat skills became like breathing. Something they did naturally, without having to think about it. The Samurai seeks to balance the qualities of both the warrior and the monk in his life."

Meditation and contemplation, Connor thought. *Those were almost the exact words that Fujiyama used to explain the Samurai in his study that day—that now seemed so long ago.*

Nakamura poured himself another cup of tea. "So you see, Connor-san, a warrior that pursues a greater spirituality in his life is not a contradiction. A *true* warrior is challenged to perfect his character—physical, emotional, and spiritual. This is called *Kaizen*, a process of constant, never-ending improvement."

He looked around his surroundings before continuing. "So, joining a monastery and becoming a monk is a natural outcome for the Samurai seeking to continuously improve his character."

All of this did little other than to confuse Connor.

"What has all this about character to do with fighting? It won't be any good on the battlefield," Connor grumped.

Nakamura thought for a few moments. "Perhaps a Zen story would make you understand better."

Food appeared at that moment and Nakamura waited to begin eating before continuing his enlightenment upon Connor.

The meal was strictly vegetarian and yet, even though there was no meat or fish, the meal proved to be filling and satisfying. Connor had trouble figuring out what most of the dishes were, but it did not really matter, as it was all extremely tasty.

Finally, Nakamura told his story. "Once, many years ago, a Japanese tea master was challenged to a duel by a Samurai who was trying to scare money from the tea master. As there was no way to decline with honor, the tea master resolved that he would accept the duel and die with his principles intact. So, he visited a neighboring fencing master and requested that the swordsman teach him the art of dying."

"But what does that have to do with being a Samurai?" Connor asked impatiently.

"You'll see. My story is not finished. Patience, too, is a virtue," he winked. Nakamura resumed his retelling of the tale. "The fencing master said that the tea master had a unique request, but he would grant it. But first, he asked the tea master to serve him a cup of tea. The tea master was only too glad to make tea for the fencing master, for this was most likely the last chance to practice his art."

Connor looked over at Aiko. "Like the tea ceremony you did for me?"

"Hai," she nodded.

Nakamura stirred his tea. "Now, forgetting all about the duel itself, the tea master proceeded to prepare the tea as if this was all that concerned him at the moment. The swordsman found himself deeply impressed with the tea master's concentrated state-of-mind from which all the superficial stirrings of consciousness were swept away."

Nakamura stretched out his hands in a grand gesture. "The swordsman exclaimed, 'There you are!' and told the tea master there was no need for him to learn the art of death. The tea master's present state of mind was enough for the man to cope with any swordsman."

"But did the Samurai kill him?" Connor asked, barely able to conceal his curiosity.

Nakamura held up his palm in a sign for Connor to wait.

"The swordsman instructed the tea master that when he met the Samurai, to do exactly what he had done for the fencing master. First, to think that he was going to serve tea for a guest. Next, to salute the Samurai respectfully and tell him that he was now ready for the contest. He was to take off his outer coat, fold it carefully, and then use his fan, just as he did when he served tea. Then, the tea master was to draw his sword, lift it high over his head in full readiness to strike down an opponent, and concentrate his thoughts for combat. When he attacked, he was to strike him with his sword, which would probably result in a mutual slaying."

"What happened?" Connor asked eagerly.

Nakamura laughed at Connor's eagerness. "The tea master thanked the sword master for his instruction and went to the location where he had promised to meet his opponent. He scrupulously followed the swordsman's advice with the same attitude of mind and spirit as when he was serving tea. Then, boldly standing before the mighty Samurai, he raised his sword, and the Samurai observed an altogether different person before him. The Samurai saw no opening for attack, for the tea master now appeared to him as the embodiment of fearlessness."

"So what did the Samurai do?"

"The Samurai threw down his sword, knelt upon the ground, and asked the tea master's pardon for his rude behavior."

Nakamura stared at Connor. "Without the character traits of honor, integrity, and justice, there is no warrior. Do you understand what I mean about character? That tea master had strength of character?"

Connor nodded, still processing the story and its meaning. "I guess."

"And you must remember this, Connor-san. Training in the art of war or in the martial arts without regard to character only produces a dangerous man, and for a nation, dangerous actions. Fujiyama must have taught you this if he instructed you in the code of the Samurai."

The True Samurai

"Why do you hold Fujiyama in such contempt?" Nakamura asked, his tone benevolent.

This exclamation put Connor aback. "Because he taught us the Samurai code, but he didn't *practice* it," Connor quickly replied.

"How so?"

Connor's resentment for Fujiyama boiled inside him, and he responded without holding anything back. He told Nakamura of all that had happened—the lies and deceits that made up his life. The loss of the two women he loved. His confused attempt at living the code of the Samurai and his alienation as an American and then as a half-Japanese that prevented him from living that very same code he aspired to.

Nakamura could see the all-consuming pain in the boy's eyes. As he listened to Connor's rant, he recognized the deep-seated anger in the young man's soul and why Aiko had brought Connor to him.

"What *did* Fujiyama teach you about the code?" Nakamura asked after Connor finished unburdening himself.

"He taught me its tenets." Connor numbered them off on his fingers as if from a rote assignment. "Justice, benevolence, veracity, politeness, loyalty, and honor. Loyalty and honor above all," Connor reemphasized. Fujiyama said loyalty and honor, especially to family and friends, were of the greatest importance. But Fujiyama showed none himself."

Nakamura detected that Connor was holding something back.

"So you searched for it elsewhere?"

Connor thought long and hard before answering. "Hai. With the Yakuza."

Aiko physically recoiled at the confession, but Nakamura remained steadfast.

"You joined the Yakuza, Connor–san?" Aiko asked.

"No. Not exactly," Connor shook his head. "Just spent some time with them. Thought I would finally get respect."

A long, tense pause hung in the little room until Nakamura spoke once again. "The tenets, Connor–san, you just told me were the very words of the Bushido Code. A code ultimately corrupted by the militarist and foisted upon the public as the Samurai Code."

"But—I thought they were the same?" Connor replied.

"No," Nakamura said bluntly. "The Japanese military version of bushido dictated that soldiers were expendable. Fighting for the Emperor determined that they had no identity of their own. Their individuality was simply erased." He leaned closer to the boy. "Hear me, Connor-san. If the military and nationalists taught the real bushido, the *real* Samurai code, it would teach that a Samurai must *know* oneself, not *lose* oneself. He must be in the world but not of it."

Nakamura took a sip of tea and allowed Connor to reflect upon these words for a few moments. "Connor-san, do you know what the literal meaning of the word, *Samurai?*"

Aiko interjected before Connor could form his own conclusion. "The word Samurai is written with two Chinese characters. The first means *stop enemy's sword* and the second means *gentleman.*"

Nakamura agreed. "Hai. So you see, there is nothing aggressive itself in the Samurai spirit." He paused then smiled. "And the Yakazu are no gentlemen."

Nakamura allowed this to hang in the air before continuing. He sat back in his chair and sipped at his green tea. "Benevolence and mercy, Connor-san, are part of the code of a Samurai. The Samurai, invested with the power to kill, was expected to demonstrate equally extraordinary powers of benevolence and mercy. In your case, by protecting you from the truth of your past, a painful truth that could be damaging to you, Fujiyama was exercising both benevolence *and* loyalty."

Connor mulled this over then reflected back over Goro's actions and how he abandoned Kodo. "But what of the 47 Ronin? Revenge was their duty, not mercy."

"You not only misunderstand the Samurai code, but the 47 Ronin as well."

"How?" Connor asked.

"The 47 broke the Samurai code by pursuing an unauthorized vendetta. Pursuing *revenge*. The 47 lost all sense of honor with their plans of blind vengeance."

Connor stood, then quickly sat right back down. "I don't understand."

Nakamura nodded, fully expecting the boy's response. "By killing the murderer of their Lord, they had to redeem their honor."

"Hai. Honor is honor," Connor said, repeating what Jiro had told him.

Nakamura shook his head. "Incorrect. They were expected to follow their master into death rather than face the dishonor of being a master-less Samurai—a Ronin. But instead, they decided to remain amongst the living to seek revenge, thereby publicly dishonoring them. If they had honor they would have committed *seppuku* immediately after their master's death. But they chose not to abide by this oath."

Nakamura pressed his hands together and continued. "The Ronin spent well over a year waiting and plotting for the appropriate time for their revenge. But according to proper bushido teachings, they were to attack their master's murderers *immediately* after his death. They did not. They conceived a convoluted plan to ensure they would succeed in killing their master's murderer, which is not a proper concern of a Samurai. By waiting, they improved their chances of success but risked dishonoring the name of their clan, the worst transgression a Samurai can commit. The tale of the 47

Ronin is a good story of revenge, but by no means a story of true *bushido*—of true *Samurai*."

He placed his hand upon Connor's shoulder. "Do you understand?"

"I think," Connor replied. "Maybe."

Connor noticed Nakamura exchange an awkward glance with Aiko, and sensed the monk was holding something back. But instead of challenging the old man, Connor held his tongue.

Matsumuro

Connor and Aiko arrived back in Tokyo late that night amidst a pounding rainstorm, and the two lovers returned to Aiko's room at the geisha house. The steady sound of rain against the wooden roof added to the mood of serenity.

As Connor curled beside Aiko in bed, he replayed all the words Nakamura had shared with him, trying to his best to compartmentalize the flood of emotions. As Aiko pressed closer, the touch of this exquisite young woman caused Connor to ponder, *How can it get any better than this?* As if to answer this very question, his thoughts were interrupted by a light knocking on the bedroom door.

"Hai?" Aiko said softly.

No answer. Only more knocking.

Aiko crawled out of bed and walked to the door. When she opened it, one of the other geisha's stood in the hall with a distraught expression covering her soft face. The two women exchanged hushed, anxious murmurs, then Aiko hurried back into the room.

"You must leave now, Connor-san."

Connor sat up and gave her a curious look. "What? Why?"

"My sponsor. Matsumuro. He is here." She glanced back at the door. "If he were to see you here—"

She didn't get the chance to complete her thought as a massive Japanese man with a topknot shoved his way into the room. Connor guessed the man to be a sumo wrestler, as he must have weighed well over three hundred pounds.

The sumo filled the entire doorframe with his enormous girth. He stared at Connor prone on the bed, then stood aside as a middle-aged man, neatly dressed in a pinstriped suit and impeccable leather shoes, stormed into the room. The man waved off the sumo with a well-manicured hand and approached Aiko directly.

"Matsumuro-san," Aiko said in a submissive voice, bowing deeply in front him.

Matsumuro glared at Connor. "Who is this ijin?"

"A friend, Matsumuro. Nothing more than that."

Matsumuro glanced at Connor with cold eyes, then nodded to the sumo who lumbered over and yanked Connor out of bed as if he weighed nothing. The mountain of a man slammed the boy to the hardwood floor and stomped one of his burly legs atop Connor's back, pressing him flat to the ground.

"*Matsumuro*," Aiko pleaded. "Don't hurt him. Please?"

Matsumuro stared down at Connor before turning to Aiko. "Does he pay you?"

"No. I said he was a friend."

"I see. Well, he will no longer be your *friend*," he roared and crouched down next to Connor, pressing his face to the young American and hissed. "You will never see Aiko again. Ever. If you do, I will kill you, ijin. *Do you understand?*

Connor wanted to defend his love for Aiko but what could he do with Sumo glaring down at him.

Despondence

Connor was hurting, not only from the rough handling of the sumo but also from the emptiness he felt from not being able to share Aiko's company; not only the physical connection, but the emotional one as well. But he knew it would be impossible to see her again. He was certain that Matsumuro would have him watched as long as he remained in Tokyo. And he sure as hell didn't want to cross paths with that sumo again.

Though bitter and with no options, he resigned himself to returning to Hiroshima. With a heavy heart, after he had arrived at the Hiroshima train station, Connor decided to walk from the city to the Fujiyama home to clear his head and think. He knew Fujiyama had been released from the naval hospital and returned home quite some time ago. He was still deeply confused over Fujiyama and didn't know what to say to him when they met.

A few blocks from his home, he heard a familiar voice shout to him from down the block. "Hey, Ijin," Jiro teased as he walked toward Connor. "Back from the dead, I see."

Connor grinned. "Good to see you, my friend."

"We've missed you. Or should I say, a *certain sister* of mine has."

That was the first time Connor thought of Kodo in many months. "I missed you, too, Jiro-san."

"Let's celebrate your triumphant return," Jiro said as he slapped Connor on the back. "I have a nice bottle of sake that wants to sacrifice itself. Come. Let's not keep it waiting."

Duty and Responsibility

Fujiyama sat upon a large futon in his living room, quietly reading the daily war news. The paper exulted in the successes of the Japanese military—as it did every day—turning apparent defeats into courageous victories.

Miyoko brought him a cup of hot tea and noticed the frown on her husband's face. "Bad news?"

"Not according to our *esteemed* press. But I know better." He folded the paper and tossed it aside. "Nothing but propaganda. I barely escaped the destruction of the naval base at Rabaul by U.S. carrier–based planes. Those same U.S. carrier planes also decimated the large naval base at Truk the day before. The Japanese Navy has lost two of its major naval bases in the South Pacific and *that*," he pointed toward the newspaper in front of him, "says nothing of those devastating loses."

Miyoko handed her husband his tea and knew it best to let him vent his frustration.

Fujiyama sighed and stared at a sleeve of papers on the table. "I have to leave soon."

Miyoko took a seat next to him. "When?"

"Too soon. I have to report to my ship tomorrow." He gazed up at the ceiling. "What the general public doesn't know is that our bases in the Mariana Islands have been attacked by American carrier planes. American forces are bypassing Truk and preparing to invade."

He looked at his wife. "Saipan is in the Mariana Islands. If the Americans take Saipan, they will break through the inner ring of our defenses."

"And what does that mean exactly?" Miyoko asked.

"It *means* the enemy will have a base to attack our mainland—our homes—with their new long range bombers. Saipan is within our territory. The Americans' new heavy bombers, their B-29s, have a range of 3,500 miles. The distance between Tokyo and Saipan is not even *half* that."

"Oh, Akihito. I'm frightened for the children."

He patted Miyoko's shoulder and drew her to his chest. "I know. But perhaps the Navy will succeed in defending Saipan from the Americans." He lifted her face towards his. "That's my duty and responsibility now."

He paused a moment as he reflected upon what lay ahead of him. "Each and every Japanese soldier and sailor now has a new responsibility. One that far surpasses that of serving the Emperor. Their duty now is to protect and be willing to die for their families." He drew a deep breath. "Perhaps that will make the difference. We can only hope and pray that it does."

Disgraced

Connor was drinking his second cup of sake with Jiro at the Yakuza warehouse when Sato walked in. Sato approached Connor wearing his heinous grin. "Connor, I heard you were sick."

Connor nodded. "Hai. I was in the hospital for awhile, then recuperating with family in Tokyo."

As Sato surveyed the young teen in front of him, his constant smirk never faltered. "I also hear you are half-Japanese."

Connor looked to Jiro, then back to Sato. "How did you know that?"

"Oh, we have our ways. You should know that by now," Sato replied in a conspiratorial tone.

Connor didn't know exactly how to respond. "But it doesn't change anything. I'm still an ijin in both worlds—American and Japanese."

Sato put his arm around the boy. "You're always accepted here. No matter what."

Just then, a pair of tattooed arms grabbed Connor from behind, and spun him around. Before Connor could react, *Kodo* leaned down and planted a passionate kiss on his lips.

"I'll leave you two alone," Sato laughed. "I see you have some catching up to do."

After Sato stepped away from the table, Kodo once again pressed her lips to Connor's. But after a moment, she pulled away, looking confused and even a little hurt. "Is there something wrong? I thought you would be happy to see me."

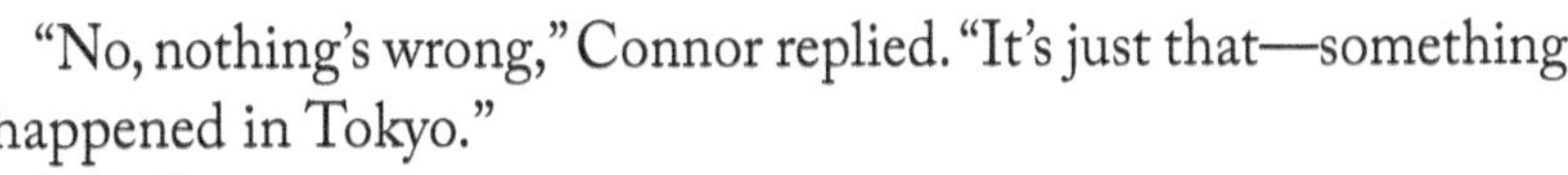

"No, nothing's wrong," Connor replied. "It's just that—something happened in Tokyo."

"Oh?"

Connor wasn't prepared to confess his love for Aiko, so instead, he replied with a different confession. "I met a Buddhist monk."

Jiro poked a playful finger to Connor's ribs. "You're turning into a Buddhist and quitting women?"

"No. Nothing like that." Connor searched for the right words. "It's just that... he told me things. Things that confused me. *Still* confuse me."

"About what?" Kodo asked.

"The 47 Ronin. The monk claims that what they did was dishonorable."

Both Kodo and Jiro bristled at the insult.

"And just who is this monk?" Jiro pressed.

"A retired admiral," Connor replied. "His name is Nakamura."

"*Nakamura?*" Jiro snapped.

"Hai. You've heard of him?"

"I know his name, and I'm told of his reputation."

"Reputation?" Connor said.

"Wait here," Jiro instructed, then walked over to Sato who was speaking with the recently arrived Goro and giving him some kind of instruction.

Jiro spoke to Sato for a moment, and when they returned to the table, Sato was less than jovial this time. "You want to know about Nakamura's reputation?"

Connor nodded.

"The man is disgraced. He was shamed in the eyes of the Emperor and lost all access to the throne," Sato stated. "He was forced out of the Navy and rank removed. So the monastery is where he hides now, ashamed to show his face." Connor, thoroughly confused by these accusations, said nothing.

Sato lowered his voice and pressed his face close to Connor's. "You want to see honor? You want to do the honorable thing? Then go with Goro tonight. The Yakazu will teach a defeatist what it means to be a traitor."

The Defeatist

The sun had already set on what turned out to be a rainy, moonless night. Goro, Kodo, Connor, and a half dozen other Yakuza, made their way quietly through the back streets of Hiroshima, and towards a residential district familiar to Connor.

As Kodo walked close to his side, Connor saw that Goro and the other Yakazu were carrying pistols or clutching heavy knives.

The driving rain made it difficult for Connor to hear Goro whispering orders to the other Yakuza. After a few minutes, they approached a small street dotted with homes and made their way down a dark back alley.

When they arrived behind a darkened home, Goro stopped and pointed at the back of the house. "There. The defeatist."

A realization of shock hit Connor as he stared over at the home—*his* home—the Fujiyama's.

"When I say fire," Goro ordered, "spray the windows of the house." He handed Connor a small pistol. "Take this. For honor."

At that moment, a sliver of light sliced into the night, and Miyoko stepped out the back door of the house.

Goro saw Connor's uncertainty, then whispered into his ear. "You give the order to shoot."

Connor lowered his pistol and backed away from Goro and the others. "No."

Goro simply raised his pistol and pressed it to the tender flesh of Connor's temple. "Give the order, Connor-san. Do it now."

The other Yakuza stood at the ready, waiting to see what Connor's next move would be.

Connor stared at Goro for a moment, the rain pounding down upon them, then bolted toward his home. "Go back inside, Mama-san! Go back inside the house!"

Goro pointed his gun at Connor's back and screamed. "Ijin Kuso yarō!"

A scream filled the night air, followed by the piercing report of a gunshot, and Connor's body hit the wet ground. He looked over his shoulder and watched Kodo, eyes wide open in distress, collapse in front of Goro. She had taken the bullet intended for Connor.

The sound of the Yakuza's gunfire brought someone else to the back door. Backlit by the light from inside the house, Fujiyama ushered his wife into the house, then stepped out onto the yard. He carried a service pistol and took aim upon the Yakuza.

"Who's there?" he bellowed into the night.

Surprise now out of the question, and confronting an armed opponent, Goro kicked Kodo's dead body to the side and ordered the Yakuza to disperse.

They were gone in an instant, disappearing into the rain and darkness.

Fujiyama raced to Connor, who knelt over Kodo's still form.

Connor stared up at his Japanese father, tears streaming down his face, mixing with the rain. "She died for me..."

Fujiyama placed his hand on Connor's shoulder. "What are you doing here, my son? Why aren't you in Tokyo?"

Connor couldn't bear to look at Fujiyama, hanging his head in shame instead.

"I was with them. I was with the Yakuza."

Confession

After the police left and a report was filed, Fujiyama and Miyoko sat with Connor in the living room.

Connor explained his time spent with the Yakazu and his reasons why. He was relieved that Suki and Kenji had gone to bed, both of his siblings unaware of what had transpired at their home. And neither Fujiyama or Miyoko said anything to them later about the evening's event.

"The Yakuza targeted you," Connor said to Fujiyama. "Why?"

"Political reasons, I gather." He studied his son for a moment. "Who gave the order to attack the house?"

"His name is Sato," Connor replied. "He's in charge of the Yakuza group."

"Sato? An Army Colonel?"

"I don't know."

"Does this man have a scar on his face?"

Connor's stunned silence was his answer.

Fujiyama raised an eyebrow. "I'm going to ask the Navy to supply some military police to watch the house for a while."

"Papa-san," Connor said. "I need to ask you something." Connor told him what the Yakazu had said about Nakamura's disgrace.

Fujiyama thought a moment before replying. "Nakamura's disgrace happened after the First War. I really don't know the details, just that he was a personal confidant and mentor of our Emperor Hirohito, but had somehow lost all his favor with the throne."

Fujiyama could see how exhausted and traumatized Connor appeared, and they had yet to discuss the death of Kodo.

As if sensing what his father was thinking, Connor looked to Fujiyama and spoke softly. "I'm very tired. I'd like to go to bed."

"Hai. We need to talk more, but now is not the time," Fujiyama agreed. "But one last thing, Connor-san. I leave first thing in the morning, and whatever you feel about me, I'm going to leave it up to you to protect our family. Do whatever is necessary to keep Miyoko, Suki, and Kenji from harm. *Anything.*" He gripped Connor's arm. "Do you promise?"

Connor took a deep, determined breath. "Hai. I will. I promise."

A Promise Kept

"**D**omo, Admiral Yamamoto," Fujiyama whispered into dawn's early morning air. He stood upon the Hiroshima Imperial Naval dock alone in his thoughts. "Domo arigato."

The Admiral and friend had kept his promise to Fujiyama. Before him, in the grey sunup mist stood the 32,000-ton *Zuikaku* fleet carrier. Known as the *Auspicious Crane*, she was one of the six aircraft carriers that participated in the attack on Pearl Harbor and a proven veteran of the Battle of the Coral Sea and Guadalcanal campaigns.

After he boarded and performed the ritual of taking command, he made his way to his cabin and was greeted with a surprise— Admiral Ugaki. "Sir! If I had known…"

"Oi. Relax my friend."

"Please, come sit," Fujiyama replied. "Would you like some tea?"

Ugaki shook his head. "What I have to say will be brief since you will be shipping out shortly." He pulled up a chair opposite Fujiyama's desk. "I'll get straight to the point. I want you back on the General Staff. I have an important mission that needs men like you."

"Sir," Fujiyama replied as he poured two cups of tea, "I was just assigned to the *Zuikaku*. Orders say the General Staff expects the Americans to invade the Marianas."

"Hai. This will be our last chance to stem the American tide. But I'm speaking of *after* that."

He accepted the proffered cup of tea and took a sip before continuing. "Captain, you know as well as I that the Americans can project their power anywhere they please. And the vehicle of that power are their aircraft carriers. Without their carriers, and the combat air support they provide, they could not efficiently island hop through the South Pacific. Their carriers have been the very key to their success and must be stopped at any cost."

"Stopped?" Fujiyama replied. "How exactly?"

"I'm forming a Special Attack Force to do just that." Ugaki finished his tea and pushed the cup across Fujiyama's desk, then said bluntly, "Gyokusai."

Fujiyama knew what that meant—*to scatter like a shattered crystal ball.* "Suicide attacks?"

"Hai. On their carriers. The only way to blunt their power." He stood up and straightened his jacket. "Please consider this once your campaign is completed."

Fujiyama stood up as well and walked around his desk. "I will think about it, sir."

Ugaki reached over and patted Fujiyama on the shoulder. "Good. And good luck against the Americans."

That afternoon, as the *Zuikaku* plowed south through the ocean towards the Philippine Sea, Fujiyama stood outside the bridge of the mighty carrier watching the young pilots joking and laughing on the flight deck. He could see they were in good spirits and ready for the coming fight.

Just then he heard a familiar voice behind him. "Commander Hiryo Fujiyama reporting, sir."

Fujiyama turned to see his son Hiryo and returned his snappy salute. "Well, this is a surprise. I wasn't aware that you were assigned to the *Zuikaku*."

"Just this morning, sir. I'm in charge of the air group."

His father gave his son a broad smile. He wanted to hug him but such an appearance would not be conductive to ship's discipline. "It's good to have you on board. And by the way, congratulations on your promotion."

Fujiyama motioned down at the pilots on the deck. "They're an eager bunch." He ran his hand over the rail in front of him marked by the cracks and pitted metal of combat. "And we have a battle-hardened ship to deliver them."

Hiryo sighed. "Eager, yes. But many of them haven't even finished their training. Those pilots—green as they come—will have to fight American pilots who are true veterans of war." He paused a moment in reflection, then looked back to his father. "Boys against men."

Fujiyama could sense his son's eagerness for the war and willingness to die for the Emperor had receded. What remained was the strict duty of a fighter pilot and his commitment to it. "They'll do their duty, none the less," Fujiyama replied. "By the way, your cousin Daiki Onaga is assigned to the ship. He's my yeoman. I believe he's in the mess hall."

Fujiyama gave his son, and now commander of the ship's air group, a steely look. "I don't have to remind you how important this mission is."

"Hai. My pilots will do their best. I'll see to that."

The Fate of the Empire

The next morning, Daiki Onaga arrived on the bridge with a dispatch for Fujiyama clutched in his hand. "Sir, we've arrived at the Mariana Archipelago just east of the Philippines. We've received a message from the Commander of the Fleet, Vice-Admiral Jisaburo Ozawa, that was sent to all ships in the fleet."

"Read it," Fujiyama replied and kept his gaze upon the sea.

Daiki focused his eyes on the dispatch. "It reads: *The fate of the Empire rests on this one battle. Every man is expected to do his utmost.*'"

Fujiyama nodded. This was it. The IJN had decided the time for the long-awaited *Kantai Kessen*—the decisive battle—had arrived. The fleet that surrounded the *Zuikaku* represented the bulk of the Japanese Navy, nearly every serviceable ship, was committed to the upcoming engagement, along with its entire naval air component.

Fujiyama stared out over the bridge and surveyed the large fleet surrounding him: Three fast fleet carriers—the *Taihō, Shōkaku,* and his *Zuikaku*—two slower carriers converted from ocean liners—the *Junyō* and *Hiyō*—four light carriers— the *Ryūhō, Chitose, Chiyoda,* and *Zuihō*—five battleships the *Yamato, Musashi, Kongō, Haruna* and *Nagato*—in addition to thirteen heavy cruisers, six light cruisers, twenty-seven destroyers, six oilers, and twenty submarines.

What did the Americans have? Fujiyama wondered, knowing full well that before you can even worry about the numbers of the enemy, you have to find him—and you hope to do so *before* he finds you.

A seaman handed Daiki another dispatch. "Sir. Orders are to launch our planes. Our scout planes have located the enemy." He presented Fujiyama with the coordinates of the American Fleet.

"Hai. Prepare to launch planes," Fujiyama ordered. "At least we have one thing in our favor," he remarked to Daiki. "The area here is dominated by the easterly trade winds which works well for our aircraft. It will give them a good headwind for take off."

✳ ✳ ✳

As the order to prepare for attack was announced over the ship, Hiryo gazed across the mess hall table to Sakio Komatsu, his wingman. "Breakfast's over, Sakio. The hunt is on!"

Sakio had trained under Hiryo on Rabual, and the two young men had become close friends. When Hiryo was assigned as air group leader, he officially asked for Sakio to join his fighter squadron and become his wingman. A kindred soul who was also a veteran of Pearl Harbor and Midway, Sakio had developed the same doubts of the war as Hiryo. But, also like Hiryo, both men acknowledged their duty and accepted it.

The two young pilots made their way to the flight deck and climbed into their Mitsubishi Zeros. Hiryo peered up towards the bridge and saw Fujiyama standing there. Father and son locked eyes for a few moments. No words were necessary. Hiryo then gave Fujiyama a hard salute and held it. Fujiyama stood rigid a moment, then returned the gesture.

Cheered on by the deck crews, the first wave of 300 planes—fighters, dive-bombers, and torpedo bombers—roared off into the strong wind towards their prime target—the American carriers. The assortment of planes eased into formations of individual squadrons, and every squadron was to hunt its individual target.

An hour out, Hiryo saw a large group of American Grumman F6F Hellcats bearing straight down at them—their attack had been discovered.

Hiryo led his squadron directly toward the Hellcats and tried

29

desperately to fight through the attacking American screen in order to reach their fleet, but the green pilots flying their Zeros were no match for the experienced Americans.

In a matter of moments, Hiryo's fighters were dropping all around him. Two Zeros next to him erupted into flames and spiraled towards the ocean. Another above him burst into pieces from the Hellcats' 20 mm cannons, showering Hiryo's plane with fiery debris. Zeros below fared no better.

A F6F Hellcat found Hiryo's plane in its gun sights and white-hot tracer bullets arched their way towards his Zero. Hiryo maneuvered into a tight turn, then twisted and turned his Zero to dodge the incoming machine gun rounds. He used everything he had learned as a veteran pilot, but to know avail.

Bullets peppered his Zero, threatening to tear it apart, when flying directly under his right wing, Sakio fired his 20 mm cannons and 7.7 mm machine guns at the American Hellcat.

The F6F literally stalled in the sky as the pilot grabbed at his neck and slumped forward. The enemy fighter turned on its back and plunged straight down into the briny ocean below, settling into a flume of white foam and flame.

Sakio swept around, waved his wings, and gave Hiryo a fast salute.

"Thanks, my friend," Hiryo said over his radio. "Now let's find the American ships."

Hiryo's sense of victory was short-lived, as the loss of so many attacking planes confirmed the fears he had expressed to Fujiyama that morning. But with little choice, he pressed on. Hiryo and Sakio's planes led what was left of the attack force and headed for the American fleet, which they could see now in the near distance.

The anti-aircraft screen thrown up by the American ships was like a curtain of death in front of them. *Ack-ack* shells burst all around them as the attacking Zeros and dive-bombers weaved in and out of the flak, lining up on their assigned ships. Hiryo and Sakio struggled to stay with the dive-bombers, who were looking for a carrier, but it was difficult to both avoid the flak and concentrate on their individual targets.

After one of their evasive maneuvers, he and Sakio found their planes positioned near several dive-bombers as they made their attack on an enemy battleship. They immediately flew cover for the dive-bombers, following them down to the deck with the *rata-tat-tat* of their machine gun fire pouring into the enemy's steel hull.

The dive-bombers released their bombs, but only one found its target.

Hiryo climbed back into the sky to a high altitude to survey the results of their attack.

To his dismay, there were far fewer planes now than when they arrived. "Squadrons. Report in," he ordered over his radio. He was aghast at the sparse replies—nearly sixty percent of the attacking group had been lost.

What remained of the squadrons returned to the fleet only to see the carrier *Shokaku* in flames and dead in the water. It was badly damaged and returning planes that had landed on the deck to be refueled for a second strike, were strewn like toys all over the deck in balls of fire.

Hiryo spotted no enemy planes in the area, and he hadn't passed any going out of the area. He surmised that the *Shokaku* had been attacked by an enemy submarine.

Ammunition and exploding bombs added to the conflagration, as did burning fuel spewing from shattered fuel lines. With the *Shokaku's* bow sliding into the sea and fires burning out of control, Hiryo could only watch helplessly as men scrambled off the side to abandon ship.

Suddenly, Hiryo's plane was rocked by an immense series of explosions below as the *Shokaku* literally blew apart.

Over his radio, he heard Sakio mumble, "Oh, God," as the 25,000-ton carrier, engulfed in flames, rolled over and slipped beneath the green waves.

Hiryo shook his head in disbelief. He flew over the *Taiho*, when he noticed the telltale sign of torpedoes in the water heading straight for their flagship.

The carrier had just launched its second wave of planes when a spread of six torpedoes plowed their way towards the carrier. Within seconds, two of the six fish hit home, rupturing one of the starboard fuel tanks.

The damage appeared minor because the *Taihō* quickly resumed regular operations launching and recovering planes.

"Does anyone see the *Zuikaku?*" Sakio asked over the radio.

"Off to your right. On the horizon," came a reply from one of the other pilots.

Hiryo looked up and saw their carrier retrieving planes. As his squadron lined up to land, Hiryo noticed a slender wake speeding towards the *Zuikaku*. "Torpedo in the water! Torpedo in the water!"

With the alert barely out of his lips, he saw Sakio break formation and dive towards the ocean, shadowing the deadly ordinance. It took only a moment for Hiryo to realize Sakio's fate.

As his wingman approached the racing torpedo, Hiryo opened fire with all his guns. Darts of water leapt around the torpedo—front, back and sides—but the weapon continued on towards its target as Sakio came closer and closer to the unstoppable menace.

When Sakio was almost on top of the torpedo, Fujiyama heard him whisper into his radio, "Sayonara, my friend."

Hiryo watched in horror as Sakio crashed his fighter into the torpedo, exploding into a ball of boiling water and fiery wreckage.

The Turkey Shoot

"Damage report," Vice-Admiral Jisaburo Ozawa ordered the yeoman on the bridge of his flagship, the *Taihō*.

The yeoman saluted and stated, "The damage seems minor, Sir. The flooding was quickly contained and both propulsion and navigation were unaffected."

"What about the leaking vapors in the hanger deck?" Ozawa said as he watched the second wave of planes take flight from the deck.

"We're trying to clear the vapors from the broken fuel tanks at this very moment, Sir. Damage control is ventilating it from the hanger deck. They're running the ventilation system full blast."

Ozawa turned around quickly and said, "Full blast? Wouldn't that spread the fumes around too quickly?"

"I don't think—"The yeoman was cut short mid-sentence when several explosions deep below the decks rocked the entire ship, followed by a large piece of the flight deck literally rising up several feet and then blowing apart into flaming wreckage.

Ozawa and the bridge personnel were knocked off their feet by the blunt force of the massive explosion. They picked themselves up only to feel the ship listing to starboard. Ozawa held onto what he could and watched the flight deck belch flames and debris into the air.

"Sir!" the yeoman yelled. "We must abandon ship!"

Ozawa said nothing, his dazed expression unreadable.

"Sir," the yeoman implored. "We must transfer your flag!"

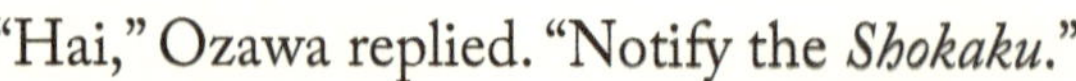

"Hai," Ozawa replied. "Notify the *Shokaku*."

It was a devastating blow to the Japanese. Two of their front line carriers had been sunk and over 600 planes destroyed with little to show for it.

"Sir?" Daiki asked. "Admiral Ozawa is aboard. He's here."

The personnel on the bridge came crisply to attention when Ozawa entered the command deck. The admiral marched around the bridge, stared out at the fleet for a moment, then asked Fujiyama for the status of his air arm.

"Perhaps a little less than sixty," he replied, reading off of his report. "Forty planes left on the *Zuikaku's* entire First Air Squadron."

"And the other squadrons?"

"About the same number of planes left in the 1st and 3rd squadrons."

Ozawa was deep in thought for several moments before responding. "Have the fleet retire to the west and refuel. We'll attack with what's left of our planes tomorrow."

As dawn broke over the ocean, the lookout on the bridge of the *Zuikaku* pointed out the glass window and shouted, "Enemy planes!" He gestured into the sky at the black flecks that grew larger and larger over the *Hiyo* several miles away.

The words barely left the lookout's lips when Fujiyama, Ozawa, and the crew of the bridge, watched two torpedoes connect to the side of their sister carrier. In a flash, secondary explosions racked the carrier and sealed her to her fate.

"There... and there!" Daiki said, pointing to the light carrier *Chiyoda*. A swarm of enemy dive-bombers were plunging at the ship. "And above us."

"Evasive maneuvers," Fujiyama ordered. "Prepare to launch our fighters."

Hearing the alarm, Hiryo's small group of less than twenty exhausted pilots hurried to the flight deck. The pilots, mostly all veterans, wearily boarded their planes, started their engines—and waited. They knew they would be sitting ducks while the huge carrier maneuvered from under the dive-bombers.

As the *Zuikaku* attempted to dodge the American bombers and torpedo planes, Hiryo saw that both the *Chiyoda* and battleship *Haruna* were hit but with little damage that he could see.

Fortunately, though *Zuikaku* sustained one direct hit, the flight deck was still serviceable.

"Turn us into the wind," Fujiyama ordered and watched as the last complement of his ship's planes took off to attack the American fleet.

It was good timing. As the last of the planes touched off from the flight deck, a huge explosion rocked the ship.

"Damage report," Fujiyama ordered.

Daiki quickly radioed to the lower decks, listened to the reports, then relayed the information to Fujiyama. "A bomb hit the aft flight deck, sir. It started a fire in the hangar, but damage control is on it."

Fujiyama looked out over the remnants of the once proud Imperial Navy Fleet, to see only the *Zuikaku* out of six fleet carriers had survived the battle.

The fleet now had only thirty-five planes left to press the attack. Fujiyama looked over at Admiral Ozawa but did not say a word. None were necessary. He could see it on his Commander-in-Chief's face. Over 600 carrier aircraft—the bulk of the Imperial Japanese Fleet's air arm—were lost. Five carriers were sunk along with six other ships damaged. All of this with very little damage to the enemy fleet.

It was nothing less than a complete disaster for the Imperial Japanese Navy.

In the Drink

"I've got eyes on the enemy fleet," Hiryo shouted over the radio. Through the wispy clouds in front of him stood battleships, cruisers, and destroyers screening the American aircraft carriers that dotted the blue ocean ahead of them.

Hiryo and his meager squadron put their Zeros into a steep dive, following the paths of the few torpedo planes and dive-bombers that hurled themselves into the barrage of flak and machine gun fire erupting from American fleet.

A few of the attacking squadron managed to make it through the artillery barrage and struck two of the American carriers—the *Wasp* and *Bunker Hill*.

"They're hit! Banzai!" Hiryo heard the victorious shouts of another pilot over his radio.

But the bombs caused limited damage as both carriers continued their steady launching of planes.

Hiryo looked around him to survey his surviving squadron. There were few planes left to return to the *Zuikaku*. He was about to give the order to break off the attack and return when his plane felt as if a large hand had grabbed its wings and rattled them violently.

His Zero immediately went into an almost uncontrollable dive headed directly for the sea. He glanced over and saw that most of his left wing had been obliterated and his plane threatened to roll over on its back at any moment.

He fought the controls to level the plane, but from his cockpit window, he watched. The ocean loomed closer and closer. At the very last moment he managed to right the plane but it was too late. His remaining wing caught the water, flipped end over end with an eruption of briny water, and slipped into the sea.

Chichibu

Around noon, after enjoying a light lunch and a walk under a sunny summer sky, Hiyakawa returned to the Imperial Palace in the heart of Tokyo. He crossed over the large moat in front of the Palace and passed through the massive ramparts of stone, guarded by ancient gnarled pines that were once used to ambush archers during feudal times.

He arrived at the Shodaibunoma, the building used as a waiting room for dignitaries and official visitors to the palace. The one story building stood broad and long, furnished in European style with the most exquisite of Japanese taste.

He passed through a red-carpeted hallway surrounded by beautiful Japanese polished wood walls and into the Emperor's office where he waited patiently to meet with Hirohito. The Lord Keeper of the Privy Seal of Japan had a standing meeting with the Emperor each week, but since falling ill, he sent his assistant, Hiyakawa, in his stead.

A diminutive Japanese bureaucrat with thinning strands of silver and black hair sat behind a formal hardwood desk in the reception area. It was unnecessary for Hiyakawa to say anything. He was well known in the Palace.

The silence between them was broken when another figure entered the waiting room at a brisk pace. Hiyakawa looked up to see Prince Chichibu stride past him.

"I'm here to see the Emperor," the Prince snapped in a tone that sounded more like an order than request.

The receptionist rose, bowed and offered no resistance to the Prince's demand. "Hai," was all the bureaucrat said.

Chichibu gave the little man a disparaging look and walked past Hiyakawa without bothering to acknowledge his presence.

A disturbing thought went through Hiyakawa's mind as the member of the Royal family past him. *It never bodes well when Chichibu needs to see the Emperor.*

✳ ✳ ✳

Chichibu strode up to Hirohito and took a seat on his right, as was customary. He took no time explaining his urgent visit.

"Japan has been bombed," he said flatly.

Hirohito recoiled in surprise. "When?"

"Last night. The Imperial Iron and Steel Works in Yawata. There was little damage as only one bomb hit the Works. You'll get the full report from the Ministry soon."

Hirohito shook his head and sighed.

"This is just the beginning, your Majesty. You should be braced for more news like this," Chichibu continued. "Though the attack emanated from somewhere in China, there will be more to come if the Americans take Saipan."

Hirohito nodded. "Go on."

"Your Majesty, if that happens, and American bombers can..." he quickly corrected himself, "...*will* reach Japan, I fear our people's fighting spirit will be greatly reduced. You must prop up resistance."

"And how do you propose I do that?"

"An edict. An Imperial order. Fight to the last breath. Suicide instead of surrender."

"But our Imperial soldiers know that," Hirohito countered.

Chichibu leaned forward in his chair. "I don't mean our *soldiers*." He narrowed his eyes and spoke emphatically. "Saipan... must... not... fall."

Hirohito did not need further explanation. "Hai. I will issue the edict."

The Edict

Prince Chichibu exited the Emperor's office, stopped, and stared straight at Hiyakawa with a malicious smile that sent a chill down the diplomat's spine.

"You can go in now," the receptionist offered to Hiyakawa, thereby interrupting the uneasy moment.

"Hai. It is your turn to speak to the Emperor." Still wearing his malevolent grin, Chichibu abruptly turned and exited.

Hiyakawa took a moment to gather himself before entering the room. Once in the Emperor's presence, he bowed deeply.

"Come. Sit my friend," Hirohito offered. "You seem troubled."

"A visit to the Palace by Chichibu always brings trouble," Hiyakawa replied. "I believe he does not have your best interests at heart."

Hirohito stared down at his hands before speaking. "He has the best interests of the Chrysanthemum Throne."

"I beg to differ, your Majesty. He only has *his* best interest at heart." Hiyakawa settled in his chair. "Your Majesty. The news reports that the sea battle in the Philippine Sea has not gone well."

Hirohito nodded. "Not well at all. Saipan is now at risk. If we lose Saipan..."

"And is this what Chichibu wanted to talk to you about?"

"Hai. He fears that if we lose Saipan, the fighting spirit of our people will be lost along with it. He is correct. We *must* maintain that spirit at all costs."

"And how exactly did Chichibu propose this to be done?"

Hirohito stood up straight as if to make a pronouncement. "It matters not what he proposed. *I* have decided. I am going to issue an Imperial Order. I will authorize Lieutenant General Yoshitsugu Saito, the commander of Saipan, to promise civilians who die an equal spiritual status in the afterlife with those of soldiers perishing in combat."

Hiyakawa had a difficult time responding. "You're ordering civilians to obey the Code of Bushido?"

"Hai. It's the only way," Hirohito replied. "Saipan is home soil and must be defended even by civilians to the last, rather than shame this Son of Heaven by surrendering."

"Your Majesty," Hiyakawa pleaded. "I ask you—I *beg* you to reconsider."

Hirohito was quiet for a moment. "There are rumors," he finally stated.

"Rumors? There are always rumors," Hiyakawa replied.

"There are those in the Palace—inside the Chrysanthemum—that want to continue this war." He searched for the right words to complete his sentiment. "I've always feared for the throne. Always. All my decisions before and during this war have been made to preserve the Chrysanthemum. Nothing more."

"Are you speaking of an overthrow of your position as Emperor?"

Hirohito nodded. "Hai. So I must find a way for us to win this conflict honorably. I will do anything I can to accomplish this."

Hiyakawa could feel the conflict in Hirohito's voice and saw that anything he could say to sway the Emperor's edict would be to no avail.

"I understand, Your Majesty," was all that Hiyakawa could manage to say.

Depose the Emperor

"Over six hundred of our planes destroyed," Prince Takamatsu, brother of Hirohito, said, holding the naval report of the battle of the Philippine Sea.

"Our air arm in the Pacific has been decimated," Prince Higashikuni, uncle to Hirohito, added despondently.

The two princes and Prince Asaka, along with the former Prime Minister Konoe, were meeting secretly with Takamatsu and Higashikuni at the Palace.

"I warned the Emperor not to go to war with America," Takamatsu said bitterly. "Yamamoto told the Naval General Staff that the Imperial Japanese Navy could not sustain hostilities for longer than a year against the United States. I believed we might have lasted two years. After Midway, I urged the Emperor to seek peace. I was ignored, and my overestimation caused a severe rift between us."

"And Tojo has publicly promised that the United States would never take Saipan," Konoe interjected. "That boast seems very unlikely now."

"What do we do?" Asaka asked.

"Depose the emperor," Takamatsu stated flatly.

"You're talking treason," Konoe replied.

"Hai. But treason may be our only option if we are to save the Empire," Takamatsu added.

"For the sake of argument, who would replace Hirohito?" asked Asaka.

Takamatsu scoffed at the question. "His son, Akihito. He is to be placed on the throne," Takamatsu replied.

"But he is just ten years old," Asaka retorted.

"Tell me something that I do not know." Takamatsu pointed at Prince Higashikuni. "Make him regent until Akihito is of age."

"But the hardline militarists?" Asaka countered. "They will surely try to fight back. They could argue that the regency was set up by traitors who are selling out their own nation."

"We will be able to impose the Regency before they're able to react," Takamatsu replied matter-of-factly. "Besides, the militarists have spent almost two decades teaching its soldiers and airmen that it's acting on the Emperor's divine will. It will be quite hard for them to turn around now and say that Japan shouldn't listen to the boy Emperor and a handful of princes. If ordinary Japanese soldiers are inclined to listen to the new Emperor, or at very least to *not* fight against him, what can they do?"

"Let's wait and see what happens to Saipan, "Higashikuni said. "Meet again then."

The group of men all nodded in silent agreement.

A Pleasant Turn of Events

"**A**nd you believe this?" I said as I slapped the latest issue of our newspaper on Sakura's desk.

"We merely report the news as it's given to us," he grumbled. "Not believe it? You of all people should know there's a difference between the two." He stuck a cigar in his mouth and lit it. "Lost engagements by our forces are not ours to comment on. Only that they were great *moral* victories."

I nodded in disgust, knowing that my editor was correct.

He picked up the paper and pointed to the headline. "So here we tell the public of our fleet returning gloriously to Okinawa after our decisive engagement with the Americans off Saipan." He paused. "Okinawa. *That's* where the news is."

"You heard something? The Americans will attack there next?"

Sakura parried my question with a sheepish smirk. "No. That's what the General Staff may think, but as for me? No."

"Oh, so now you are the great military strategist?" I mocked. "You know better than the General Staff?"

"No," he snapped. "I don't know military strategy, but I do *know* people." He walked around his desk and past a wall adorned with framed front pages of the newspaper. "This paper was built on sensational news and scandals. They were our bread and butter before the war drove them off the front page. But that doesn't change what we know about people."

"Okay. Fine. So what do we know about the Americans?"

"Like many of our own generals, Douglas McArthur is an egotist. He promised the Filipinos that he would return. And he *will* keep his word." Sakura slammed his hand against the wall. "The Philippines are next, and you're going there to report on its defenses."

Sakura noticed my pleased reaction to his declaration, then quickly nipped it in the bud. "And don't even think about pursuing that foolish treasure hunt theory of yours," he roared. "Get in there. Report the facts. And get back here as soon as possible. Got it?"

Salvation

The shark appeared just before dusk.

The lustrous dark gray and black striped predator circled Hiryo from a distance with broad strokes of its massive tail, silently assessing its prey. But with each pass, the fifteen-foot tiger shark came closer and closer attracted to Hiryo's bleeding body.

Hiryo had managed to extricate himself from his sinking Zero before it slipped below the waves and could take him along with it. His body was bruised and bloodied, and small trickles of blood spread into the water—but not so small to avoid the notice of the swimming menace.

Now, several hours later, the large predator displayed caution by swimming twelve feet from Hiryo in ever-smaller, concentric circles. But the smell of blood became too enticing, and a primitive urge to devour a helpless meal proved too instinctive.

Seemingly making a decision, the tiger shark came at Hiryo in a sudden flurry—jaws wide open, displaying a maw of razor-sharp, white teeth.

Hiryo kicked at the shark, punched the water and screamed with a desperate fury. He tried to locate his knife at his side, but every time he lowered his arm, the shark came at him again.

This went on for several minutes, slowly sapping Hiryo's strength. Near exhaustion, his resistance grew weaker with each passing moment. He didn't know how much longer he could keep the hungry predator at bay.

The tiger shark seemed to sense his flagging will and made one last thrust at Hiryo, raising its head above the water and prepared to grab its prey by the neck and drag him under.

Just as the shark broke water and was about to clamp his jaws around Hiryo's throat, Hiryo raised his hands in one last desperate attempt to ward the beast off, when *boom, boom, boom*—the report of gunfire erupted behind him and the shark's head blew apart in a spray of blood and flesh.

Hiryo peered above the swell of the ocean to see, not more than a few feet over his shoulder, a Japanese fishing boat, with two men clutching rifles and waiting to see if another shark would appear.

"Rest," an old Chamorros woman instructed Hiryo. The old woman, was dressed in a white cotton blouse with dark brown pants, worked diligently on Hiryo's wounds, occasionally pushing her jet-black hair back from her weathered, dark brown face.

"Where am I?" he asked. But the old woman kept silent and, instead, tended to his wounds.

He was about to ask again when a man entered the hut. He was thin and wiry and wore a loose top and brown dingy pants. Hiryo recognized him as one of the men from the fishing boat.

Without so much as an introduction, the man spoke in broken Japanese. "You stay here until we bring soldiers. They take you back to where you come from."

"I'm a navy pilot," Hiryo answered before asking once again, "Where am I?"

"In our village," the fisherman replied. "Rest. We make contact with your army soon."

A few days later, his wounds slowly healing, Hiryo heard the rumble of distant thunder and a frantic commotion outside of his hut. He walked out to find a Japanese lieutenant with a squad of infantrymen heading towards him. They were a ghastly sight. Dirty, disheveled, and emaciated. They looked like they arrived from hell.

And hell it was.

"Commander," the officer said, throwing Hiryo a salute. "I'm Lieutenant Wantanabi. The villagers informed us they fished you out of the sea."

Hiryo returned the salute. "Where am I, Lieutenant? What island is this?"

"You are on Saipan, Sir. And in the middle of the American invasion." He pointed to his right and then behind him. "That's canon fire. Don't know if it's theirs or ours."

"Your squad looks to be in bad shape."

"Hai. Supplies are low. We've been forced to eat what we can find. Mainly field grass and tree bark." He gestured toward his men, whose uniforms hung on them like they were two sizes too large. "You're a navy pilot. When will our Navy supply us here on the island?"

Hiryo shook his head. "I'm sorry to say that they won't be."

"What?"

"Our naval power has suffered a terrible blow. Worse, our naval air power has been decimated." Hiryo paused, wishing he had better news to report. "I doubt there will be any naval support."

Wantanabi wasn't surprised. In fact, the man had suspected as much, but not to such a drastic degree. "Before your fleet arrived, we were told that one freighter containing supplies was sunk and the second damaged by enemy action. The American submarines took their pound of flesh, too."

Hiryo nodded his agreement. "Hai, that they did."

Wantanabi straightened his weary back, rubbed at the stubble upon his chin. "If what you say is true, then we must get you off this island. I will find a way to get you to headquarters." He gazed out over the terrain. "But we have to move fast before the enemy cuts us off from our lines. They've already cut our forces off south of the island and taken Aslito airfield."

Wantanabi nodded to his men, and the ragtag group started their move out of the village. He slung his automatic rifle over his shoulder and pulled out his sidearm. "Here," the Lieutenant offered. "Take my pistol. You're going to need it."

Hiryo accepted the pistol, then before following after Wantanabi and his men, he excused himself. "Wait one minute." He hurried back into his hut and bowed to the old woman that tended his wounds. He knelt down, pulled the knife from his side and held it out to the old woman. "Domo arigato."

Saipan

As the fatigued squad made their way towards the Japanese lines, Hiryo realized that Saipan was no ordinary coral islet. "This island is massive," Hiryo remarked to Wantanabi.

"Seventy–two square miles," Wantanabi stated casually, "varying from flat cane fields to unforgiving swamps, to steep, breakneck cliffs and—to *that*." The Lieutenant pointed over a ridge toward a fifteen-hundred-foot high mountain that dominated the island. "Mount Tapotchau. That's where the Army and Navy headquarters bunkers are located," he said with a cigarette dangling from his lips.

"It looks pretty formidable," Hiryo remarked.

"General Saito has organized our troops into a defensive line across the island, anchored on Mount Tapotchau in hopes we can keep the Americans at bay." He motioned towards the west. "We'll head inland. Our forces have probably set up defenses in the hilly terrain ahead."

✳ ✳ ✳

Before dawn, the sky was dotted with star shells lighting the battlefield below them. In the distance, the rumble of artillery continued loud enough to have kept Hiryo awake most of the previous night. Hiryo's entourage had found shelter at the base of Mount Tapotchau in preparation for the climb to Navy and Army Headquarters.

Over the next few hours, the small band of men worked its slow and painful way into the maze of ridges and gullies that formed the foothills of Mount Tapotchau.

Stopping near the top of a small ridge, the squad was permitted to rest for a brief few moments. Wantanabi stared through his binoculars, surveying the area before them, occasionally chasing dirty stands of hair from his eyes. "I think we're still behind our lines," he said to Hiryo. "How are you doing?"

"Holding up," Hiryo replied in a weary voice.

"So what kind of pilot are you exactly?" asked Wantanabi as he dropped the binoculars from his eyes.

"Fighter pilot. Zeros."

"Been at it long?"

"Pearl Harbor, Midway, Guadalcanal, and now here."

"A survivor, huh? Like me." He looked again through his binoculars. "With luck, you will meet your commanding Admiral."

"Nagumo. Hai, I've met him once before," Hiryo replied. "At my graduation from flight school. I was witness to a rather heated discussion with him. He was discussing battleships verses aircraft carriers with Captain Minoru Genda who gave the commencement speech. Genda said the future of warfare would be with the aircraft carrier. Nagumo disagreed."

"And who won the argument?"

Hiryo shrugged. "Pearl Harbor did."

Wantanabi slapped him on the shoulder and laughed. "We'll get you through this and up in the air again..."

But a mechanical rumbling of the ground cut off his words.

Roaring out of the darkness from down the hill and a quarter mile on their left, forty or so Japanese Type 95 light tanks rumbled through the jungle with a regiment of infantry walking closely behind.

"Oi!" Wantanabi said in stunned amazement. "That is the largest tank attack I've ever seen!"

They were in the perfect spot to watch the assault as the whole panorama was spread out before them. From their vantage point, they could see the tanks firing while moving down the face of the hill as precisely as if they were going down a stepladder.

Type 95's 37mm cannons fired at a breakneck pace at the American tanks coming up to confront them. A bedlam of cannon discharges and machine gun tracers saturated the air as tanks on both sides were hit and set afire.

A Japanese tank was hit and the turret blew clear off while an American tank's crew frantically tried to escape their own burning monster. A Japanese infantryman threw a grenade into the open turret, quickly ending their attempt to flee.

Hiryo watched in stunned disbelief at the ferocious scene before him. The madness of the battle silhouetted more tanks churning out of the flickering shadows.

For a while, the American armor-piercing projectiles passed clean through the lightly armored Japanese tanks, leaving a few of them in action. The Marines tankers soon realized what was happening and switched to high explosive 75mm ammo to make their hits more effective. The results were swift and staggering. Three quarters of the Japanese tanks sat on the battlefield as smoldering hulks.

Hiryo huddled on the ground in stunned silence at the carnage inflicted by the Americans until Wantanabi ordered them to keep moving up the mountain.

A Change of Belief

Shortly before dark on the sixth of July, Wantanabi and what was left of his squad reported to Colonel Isoroku. As they approached the field headquarters, Hiryo found himself shocked at what he observed.

Severely wounded soldiers who were unable to walk sat slumped in a circle and were systematically shot by their commanding officers. Upon completing their tasks, some of these very same officers turned their pistols on themselves and committed suicide.

"This is the end," Wantanabi whispered to no one in particular as he continued to watch the horrid scene.

But it wasn't the end. Not yet. There was more horror to come.

"Lieutenant Wantanabi," a major roared. "Join that group there and await orders."

Wantanabi saluted and walked towards a ragtag cluster of soldiers sitting on the ground in the fading daylight. It was a sobering sight. Every man able to walk was armed with whatever weapons were available. There were not enough rifles to go around, so some of the men carried sticks, rocks, or whatever they could find.

Wantanabi, exhausted from a week of stress, dehydration, and hunger, knew instinctively what was to come, and he resigned himself to that fact.

He closed his eyes and immediately slipped into a fitful sleep.

"Sir. We are assembling."

Wantanabi wiped the sleep from his eyes, stared up at the private that stood over him, then followed the soldier to an assembly area.

A group of twelve men, each holding a great red flag, stood in front of nearly three thousand of the remaining able-bodied troops.

Hiryo, from a safe position, watched in stunned fascination.

Then suddenly, thousands of cries of *banzai* filled the air as Japanese officers came forward, drew their swords and waved them in violent circles over their heads.

More cries of *banzai* along with the blasts of a bugle came from amidst the troops as they charged forward like madmen, drunk on sake and beer, led by two hundred officers waving swords and yelling at the top of their lungs. In front of this charging mass, the group of soldiers that held aloft the large red flag led the vanguard in a dramatic pageant.

Behind them came the fighting troops charging with grenades, bayonets, swords and knives, flinging themselves toward the enemy defenses located down the hill. And perhaps most incredibly of all, hundreds of hobbled men on crutches and scarcely armed, charged forward as well.

The final convulsive effort of the Japanese had begun.

Hiryo watched in horrific awe as bullets whizzed past Wantanabi as he ran. The bugler who ran beside him, abruptly stopped sounding his horn and fell dead to the ground—a bullet had gone straight through his bugle and exited out the back of his neck.

The hoard of Japanese soldiers overran the enemy positions. Thousands were killed in bloody hand-to-hand combat.

Hiryo chanced a higher view from his safe position looking for Wantanabi. He saw a spray of bullets that looked like a swarm of insects swirling around Wantanabi as deafening screams filled his ears. The air reeked of death and gunpowder. A human wave of crazed Japanese soldiers, hell bent on killing, pushed forward—kill or be killed. The Japanese troops seemed like savage animals—beasts, devils, not human at all—with the singular thought: *kill, kill, kill.*

As the din of battle peaked, Hiryo thought the charge had worked. The enemy's return fire had subsided, and their guns were being overrun.

But that thought quickly vanished from his mind.

Enemy artillery opened up and fired at point-blank range at the charging troops, mowing down hundreds of soldiers in front of Wantanabi like tall grass.

What was left of the men was cut to pieces by the short-range shelling of the U.S. Army artillery. But the crazed soldiers wouldn't stand down or retreat. Instead, they advanced over their own dead—heaped three and four high—running over their comrade's fallen bodies.

Over this mayhem, Hiryo saw Wantanabi stop his charge and move towards one of his men who was waving a bloody stump of an arm in the air, gasping and pleading for help. As Wantanabi stopped and kneeled next to the bloody soldier, a piece of shrapnel slice into him.

Wantanabi toppled to the ground and lay there a moment, more in shock than pain, as the shrieks of wounded soldiers and deafening gunfire filled the air around him. Wantanabi finally glanced down to check his injury. What he found instead was that his right leg and left foot had been blown completely off.

Hiryo felt compelled to go help Wantanabi who laid upon the ground. Finally, the banzai charge subsided, and an eerie silence enveloped the killing field, with the only sound being the moans of wounded and dying men around him.

When Hiryo reached him, Wantanabi only stared up into sky. A strange calm swept over him, thoughts of home, then he slipped into the sleep of the dead.

After the banzai charge, Sergeant Yokoi led Hiryo north as the enemy pressed forward. Thousands of Japanese civilians to assemble in the area with the Edict of the Emperor rattling in their heads.

In direct contrast to the breathtaking views of the ocean and the hills of Northern Saipan that opened before them, Hiryo watched the pitiful parade of civilians as they marched north away from the fighting. Leprosy, dengue fever, extreme cases of elephantiasis plagued many of them. Hiryo noticed most of the civilians were essentially walking skeletons, as they had no nourishment for days on end, and many others suffered from shock caused by the shelling and bombing. And because of pre-invasion propaganda that had been distributed by the Japanese to citizens of the island, many natives feared being tortured and maimed if captured by the Americans.

Hiryo shook his head and could only stare in disbelief. "Civilians caught in a war that was not of their making," he whispered to himself.

Yokoi ignored Hiryo's remark.

As they approached the cliffs, Hiryo stepped to the edge of a precipice and watched in mounting horror as men, women, and children waded out into waters below in a lemming-like procession, allowing the tide to pull them deeper into the ocean. Other civilians, who stood aside him on the high cliffs, flung themselves into shark-infested waters. And worse yet, young women tossed their children into the ocean below and then followed their husbands and brothers in suicidal plunges.

"We should do something," Hiryo cried to Yokoi. "This is madness! *Madness!*"

"And what do you expect me to do? This is an Imperial Edict," Yokoi replied, void of emotion. "Those mothers are the pride of Japanese women. The finest act of the Showa period." His eyes glazed over as if possessed by the heavens. "These instances of bravery emit brilliant flashes of light—acts without equal in the history of our country."

Hiryo looked at his escort in disgust.

But not all followed their fellow citizens into death. Small groups of the islanders backed away from the void, preferring to risk capture and American treatment to that of death. Hiryo knew that it was pointless to argue against such fanaticism, but as he opened his mouth to disagree, an explosion of gunshots and grenades erupted behind them.

"Down!" Yokoi shouted. "Enemy fire!"

Hiryo dove to the ground then peered cautiously in the direction of the pandemonium. If he thought he had seen the last of the mayhem, he was badly mistaken. Those islanders that attempted to push their way past the throng of those bent on suicide were stopped by a small group of Japanese soldiers.

"Good," Yokoi remarked. "The soldiers will not allow anyone to disobey the Edict. No one will be permitted to surrender."

The deafening sound of more gunshots and definitive commands from the Japanese soldiers filled Hiryo's ears. Those who would not obey were mowed down by rifle fire and savage beheadings by the officers. As a small mob of fleeing civilians attempted to escape, soldiers lobbed grenades at their feet, ripping entire families apart.

The bloodletting of the defenseless island residents was abruptly halted by the screaming sound of incoming artillery. Shells landed amongst soldiers and civilians alike, who made a run toward a nearby cave.

"We follow!" Yokoi yelled over the artillery fire. "To the cave."

Hiryo sprinted towards the cavern, head down, praying he would make it to the opening before he, too, was slaughtered.

Madness

Hiryo, light-headed from the sweltering heat and nearly out of breath, ran into the mouth of the cave to the welcoming relief of the cool air inside.

The cave was small with a low-hanging ceiling, and felt claustrophobic. Adding to the claustrophobia and chaos was the fact that over a dozen civilians had followed closely behind him.

One of civilians was a cultured elderly woman, obviously an aristocrat—probably the wife of a high ranking officer on the island. She was dressed in traditional Japanese clothing—a brilliant kimono, a broad sash around her waist, and hair combed perfectly. Despite the circumstances, the woman stood straight, proud, and seemingly unafraid.

"Out!" ordered Yokoi to the group of civilians. "Out of the cave. Go to the cliffs," he barked, waving his pistol at the small group.

Hiryo had enough of this madness. "Stop!" he snapped at the sergeant. "Leave these people alone."

"I can not—*will* not do that. They are to leave and fulfill the Emperor's edict—or they die here." Yokoi waved his pistol in the direction of the huddled civilians.

The cries of the women and small children echoed through the cave as they pressed behind the cultured, elderly woman in hopes that her caste would protect them.

It didn't.

"You!" Yokoi barked, pointing his gun at the proud woman. "You

are first." He grabbed her by the sash and dragged her towards the cave entrance.

"Stop!" Hiryo shouted, and drew the sidearm given to him by Wantanabi. "I order you to stop!"

Yokoi turned and snarled at Hiryo. "Traitor!" As he raised his pistol towards Hiryo, Hiryo reacted quickly and without hesitation. He shot the sergeant point blank in the shoulder.

Yokoi's eyes widened as he stood there in shock, his pistol still raised and unwavering, then aimed his weapon at Hiryo.

Hiryo responded by putting a bullet dead center through the sergeant's forehead. The sergeant collapsed on the floor of the cave—a shocked look plastered across his face.

Hiryo had one mission remaining—get to Nagumo's headquarters as soon as possible. He left the civilians to the safety of the cave and headed towards the bunker Yokoi had pointed out.

As he stepped outside, he felt relief—the shelling had ceased. Whether it was from Japanese or American artillery, he didn't care. It was a respite, and he used the opportunity to reach the Nagumo's cave.

When he arrived at the Naval Command bunker, he identified himself and was immediately ushered in to see the Admiral.

Nagumo was sitting at a makeshift desk made of sticks and boards that lacked the prestige of something befit for an Admiral of the Imperial Navy.

Hiryo could see this was not the Nagumo of Pearl Harbor and Midway. The man before him was a shell of his former self. His tired eyes projected more than just fatigue. It was resignation. No longer the confident officer that lead Hiryo and so many Imperial Navy pilots in the attacks on Pearl Harbor and Midway. Here was a man now haunted by an American Fleet out to settle the score.

"Commander Hiryo Fujiyama reporting for duty, sir," he said, giving the snappiest salute he could muster.

Nagumo looked up from his desk at Hiryo and said in a bare whisper, "There is no duty here for you, Commander."

An aide approached and stood silently awaiting permission to speak. After Nagumo nodded his approval, the aide said, "Sir. Your sub is here. They are waiting."

Nagumo shook his head. "No. I am finished here." He pointed to Hiryo. "Take this pilot to the sub. We need pilots now more than dishonored Admirals." He returned his attention to a tattered pile of papers upon his desk and didn't bother with formally dismissing his aide and Hiryo.

Hiryo would learn later that Nagumo would commit hari-kari soon after his departure. Killing himself was the only honorable act to perform in order to pay for his defeat.

Family Coup

Hiyakawa was shocked—nearly speechless—and it took him a moment to form his response.

"Are you sure, your Excellency?"

Marquis Koichi Kido, Lord Keeper of the Privy Seal of Japan, nodded his head. "It is true. Some of the Princes and Konoe are planning a coup. They plan to overthrow the Emperor and replace him with his young son, Akihito."

"I...I can't believe it," Hiyakawa stammered.

Kido shook his head. "Saipan's fall has brought great strife to the Chrysanthemum Throne. It must be protected."

"What do we do?" Hiyakawa asked.

"The question is what will *you* do."

"Me?"

"You are a distant cousin of the Imperial Family. I think you should discreetly meet with them and tell them what we know. Convince them to cancel their plans."

"Yes. I see," Hiyakawa replied. "I'll arrange a meeting immediately."

"Will Kido inform the Emperor?" Prince Takamatsu asked as he paced the floor of his home outside the Palace.

"We hope that will not be necessary," Hiyakawa replied. "Or, at the very least, tell him your plans were canceled."

Takamatsu snapped toward the little diplomat. "The war was

lost with the loss of Saipan! Its loss has opened the way to the homeland islands!"

"I understand."

"And hiding such a fact from the population is no longer possible," Takamatsu spewed with unchecked rage. "The news of mass suicides of the Saipan civilians has been devastating. It was a sign of defeat—not the spiritual enhancement as the militarists claimed."

Hiyakawa said nothing and waited for Takamatsu to calm down.

"And what does Kido expect us to do?"

"If the Emperor removed Tojo as Prime Minster," Hiyakawa proposed, "would that satisfy you and the others?"

"No. It would not," Takamatsu replied. "But what other choice do we have? It will have to do."

"I suspected as much," the Emperor said with the tone of great resignation. "And from my own family of all places."

"Your Majesty," Kido reverently replied. "If you were to remove Tojo as Prime Minister, you could head off the intended coup."

Hirohito went silent for some time before responding. "And with whom would they be satisfied?"

"Their plans were to make Prince Higashikuni regent."

The Emperor shook his head. "No. That's impossible. If the war continues to go badly, I do not want the Chrysanthemum Family to be blamed. The Prime Minister *must* be someone outside the family."

The two men sat in contemplative silence for a few moments. Finally, the Emperor spoke. "I will appoint Admiral Kantaro Susuki as Prime Minister. I will ask General Tojo for his resignation today. Inform Prince Takamatsu of my decision."

Hiyakawa bowed and left the Emperor's presence, relieved of the burden that had been foisted upon him. But Hiyakawa knew the war would go on, not just because the military wished it, but because now it was a reflection of the *Imperial Will.*

Undersea Cruise

Hiryo looked upon a clear, balmy night sky from the bridge of the I-400-class submarine. He'd seen this kind of moonless night over a calm ocean before as a flyer on aircraft carriers.

"How do you like life on a submarine, Commander?" asked Isamu Yanagi, Captain of the boat.

Hiryo found that he was able to grin, despite his circumstances. "Up here, away from the smell of diesel oil and human sweat down in that sardine can of a hull, it's not bad."

Yanagi laughed. "One hundred and forty-four men in this *sardine can* as you call it, can be pretty cramped quarters if you're not used to it." The Captain gazed out over the sea that churned softly all around them. "The water is remarkable calm. We'll make good time here running at night. Should make Okinawa in four or five days."

"You're not concerned about enemy planes?" Hiryo asked.

"Darkness is one of our best allies. It's generally safe at night, which gives us a chance to charge the batteries for tomorrow. Then we run underwater during the day." He waved his hand over the ocean in front of him. "The Pacific now is an American lake. We have to be careful. Why don't you go below and get something to eat," he added.

"If you don't mind, I'd like to stay out here for a while longer."

"Suit yourself," the Captain replied and slipped through the hatch at his feet.

"Ship bearing 170 degrees," barked the sonar operator over the boat's intercom. "Sounds like a freighter."

Captain Yanagi quickly finished his breakfast in the galley and made his way to the conning tower. "Up periscope," he ordered. "Have Commander Hiryo join us in the conning tower as well."

A few moments later, Hiryo squeezed himself into the conning tower's small space. Yanagi continued peering through the periscope, then motioned for Hiryo to take a look.

Hiryo placed his eyes on the scope and saw the outline of an approaching ship. "What kind of vessel?"

"Don't know for sure. Could be a freighter."

"Or a destroyer? Should we dive?"

Yanagi shook his head. "No. It doesn't carry the shape of a destroyer. Let's get to the bridge so we can take a closer look."

As Yanagi and Hiryo joined the lookouts on the bridge, the sub continued to plow silently through the night, and closer to the ship in question. From this vantage point, the large ship was much easier to see even in the dark night. The vessel was painted all white with a red cross on its side.

"A hospital ship," Hiryo remarked. "Ours or theirs?"

"Theirs."

A sickening thought quickly flashed through Hiryo's mind. *Is Yanagi going to attack it? Has the Imperial Navy succumbed to the abhorrent behavior of the Army?*

Yanagi leaned over and barked into the intercom to his right. "Full right rudder," he commanded. "We'll give her a wide berth. Don't want us to be noticed."

Three days out from Okinawa, running at a steady twelve knots underwater, the sonar operator reported another contact. "Bearing. Distance." Yanagi ordered as he positioned himself above the periscope.

"Bearing 315 degrees. Looks like 7,500 meters to contact."

"Up scope," Yanagi said and the long tube arose, bringing the eyepiece to his chest-level.

His executive officer, Lieutenant Commander Ito Kamogi, positioned himself on the opposite side of the periscope and read aloud the bearing and distance to target. "Bearing 315. Distance to target, 7,000 meters."

"Down scope," Yanagi said.

"Sir?" asked Kamogi.

A thin grin spread across his face. "An enemy tanker. A beauty. Fifteen thousand tons."

Yanagi noticed Hiryo appear in the tower. "Come. Take a look."

Yanagi swung the periscope around and Hiryo looked through the eyepiece. "Theirs?"

"Hai."

"Are we going after it?"

"That's right." He barked into the intercom. "Sonar, what's the bearing?"

"Steady as before, Captain."

"Ten degrees rudder," Yanagi said. "That should put us in position to strike the target. Flood tubes one, three, two and four. Stand by for observation."

"Bearing 315," Kamogi reported from the other side of the periscope. "Distance to target, 5,000 meters."

"Good. Maintain speed of 8 knots," Yanagi ordered.

"Bearing 315. Mark," Kamogi said.

"Open outer doors," Yanagi commanded. "Maintain speed. Generated range?" he said into the intercom.

"4,500 meters," the sonar operator replied.

"Final bearing?"

"Bearing mark 315," Kamogi reported.

"Down scope. Fire one!" the Captain ordered.

"One fired," Kamogi said.

"Fire three!"

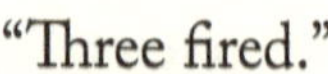

"Three fired."

"Fire two!"

"Two fired."

"Fire four!"

"Four fired."

"Time to target?" Yanagi asked.

"One minute," Kamogi replied.

Silence dropped over the tower as the crew waited for the sixty seconds to pass by.

Then, a sound that Hiryo could only describe as a rolling freight train shook the sub. A roar of celebratory cheers erupted from below.

"Up scope," Yanagi ordered and gave a long look. He adjusted the periscope towards Hiryo. "Take a look. Something you pilots will *never* see from above."

Hiryo peered through the eyepiece and saw a U.S. tanker engulfed in flames, and while he stared through the periscope, two more torpedoes hit the crippled ship. "That's how it's done, Commander," Kamogi said proudly.

But the celebration was cut short by an anxious call from the sonar man. "High speed screws coming at us fast!"

Yanagi swung the periscope back and looked through the eyepiece—an American destroyer was bearing down on them. "Down scope," barked Yanagi. "Rig for depth charges. Make depth one hundred feet." He flashed a look at Hiryo. "You better find something to hold on to. It's going to get rough."

As Hiryo nodded, a pinging sound, one he never heard before, penetrated his ears. "What's that pinging?"

"The destroyer," Kamogi replied. "He's searching for us."

"Right rudder fifteen degrees," Yanagi ordered as the pinging from the destroyer pressed on. "Sonar?"

There was a long, silent pause before sonar reported over the intercom, "He corrected his approach. Still bearing down on us, sir."

"Right full rudder!" Yanagi barked.

The amount of time between each ping grew shorter and shorter.

"Depth charges in the water!" sonar reported.

"Dive to one hundred and fifty feet," Yanagi ordered.

A few moments passed before Hiryo heard a metallic bang as shock waves from the depth charges engulfed the sub's hull. Then, a much louder boom followed as an explosion violently rocked the submarine back and forth.

Hiryo gripped a handrail and glanced over at Yanagi, who stood expressionless, showing no emotion whatsoever. "The closer the depth charge, the closer together the bang and the boom are," Yanagi stated flatly. "When the sounds become simultaneous, that might be the last sounds we'll ever hear."

Hiryo's face blanched white.

"But that's not going to happen on my watch, Commander," Yanagi said. The lights in the tower began to flicker on and off, and pipes overhead burst, spraying cold water like mini-geysers.

Crewmembers scrambled to cut the water from the fractured pipes when a depth charge exploded right outside the conning tower, hurling Hiryo back against the bulkhead, then through the hatch at his feet. He landed at the bottom deck of the conning tower, instantly snapping his leg below the knee.

"Get Commander Hiryo to sick bay," Yanagi commanded before shouting into the intercom. "Damage report!"

"Forward torpedo room flooding," came the reply. "And the engine room is taking on water, sir."

"Pumps?" Yanagi asked.

"Doing their best, sir."

"Sir," Kamogi shouted over the calls of the other men. "We're sinking."

"All stop! Blow all safeties!" Yanagi ordered.

"Depth one-eighty feet," Kamogi said as he watched the depth gauge dip. "Two hundred feet. Two-twenty. Dropping fast. Now approaching safe depth. Three hundred feet, Captain."

"All engine back!" Yanagi ordered. "Emergency power."

But the boat continued to descend deeper.

"Four-fifty," Kamogi sated.

"Blow all main ballasts!" ordered Yanagi as the lights in the ship went dark.

"Aft engine reports major flooding," Kamogi said. "Need to shut it down, Captain"

"No. Keep them running at back full."

Kamogi looked at the depth gauge and said bluntly, "Approaching six hundred feet." After a few moments of agonizing silence, he reported, "We're holding at six hundred feet, Captain."

Then, "We're rising, sir! We're going up!"

"Bring us to the surface!" Yanagi shouted. "Sonar report?"

"No contact. Sir," came the thankful reply. "I think they're gone."

The Philippines

I landed in Manila on a mid-September morning amidst torrential rains as it was the monsoon season in the Philippines.

The relentless onslaught of rain caused the temperature to feel cool, but it was still muggy from the high humidity, and my linen shirt and trousers stuck to my torso like a second skin.

I hailed a cab at the airport and checked into my hotel for a highly anticipated shower. After a change of clothing, I called the main desk and asked to be connected to the Public Relations Office at the Imperial Army Headquarters there in the city.

"Public Relations. Major Sotomura speaking. May I help you?"

"Good afternoon. My name is Yoshihara Koga, and I'm a war correspondent with the *Tokyo Nichinichi Shimbun*. I've just arrived in Manila and my editor—"

"Hai. We've been informed," he interrupted. "Where are you staying?"

I told him the name of the hotel.

"Be downstairs in thirty minutes," he replied curtly. "You will be picked up then."

That didn't give me much time, so I visited the lobby bar to get a drink or two in order to try and unwind from the long flight from Tokyo.

Two cold San Miguel beers later, I grabbed my briefcase and headed outside the hotel. And exactly thirty minutes after speaking with the public relations office, an Army staff car pulled up. I was asked to present my identification, and after my driver was satisfied with my ID, I hopped in.

It was a short trip to Imperial Army Headquarters, and I was in for a surprise when I arrived. On the wall outside the main entrance, a mounted plaque displayed the name of the Commanding Officer of the Philippines, General Tomoyuki Yamashita.

An Army Captain standing next to the door saw the expression of surprise on my face. "You know the *Tiger of Malaysia*"

I nodded. "Hai. I was there when he took Singapore."

The Captain nodded knowingly. "Not only a great man, but a great General. He replaced General Kuroda as Commanding Officer a short time ago."

I smiled politely, careful not to display my real feelings toward General Yamashita, and asked, "Where can I find the Army Public Relations Office?"

"Down the hall and to your right."

When I arrived at the office, the pressroom was empty except for a lone reporter.

"Sign in," the reporter said pointing to an unattended reception desk. He was a thin Japanese man sporting a thin mustache riding upon his upper lip and was dressed in a light tan suit, matching tie, and a cotton fedora.

I walked over to the desk and signed in on the registration form then took a seat next to the middle-aged gentleman.

"The corporal at the desk will be back soon," he informed me. "We're being taken north of the city and shown the defenses for the coming invasion."

"You think the Philippines are the next target of the Americans?"

"Hai. Guaranteed." He extended a boney hand. "My name is Yasuda."

"Koga," I replied and shook his hand.

The corporal assigned to the reception desk entered. "Follow me. There's a truck outside waiting for you both." Yasuda and I gabbed our briefcases and followed the corporal out the door to an Army truck filled with a squad of soldiers.

"What's this?" I asked the corporal as I pointed toward the heavily armed men.

"Your escort," the corporal coolly replied. "We'll be moving through some dangerous areas."

I turned to Yasuda with a questioning look on my face. He nodded, "Guerrillas."

I had heard rumors of guerrillas fighting the Japanese occupation forces in the jungles and hills, but no hard news about them. Not surprising since any resistance by the Filipinos to their participation in the Greater East Asia Co-Prosperity Sphere would most definitely be censored.

After all, we were supposed to be one great big happy Asian family.

As I did not know Yasuda's political feelings on the war, I didn't share my sarcasm. I simply shrugged my shoulders and climbed into the back of the truck with our armed escort.

Captured

The rain finally let up, was replaced with the hot sun, and the humidity increased to unbearable levels the deeper we rode into the jungle. I wiped my brow with a handkerchief and marveled at Yasuda. The man wasn't sweating at all.

When he noticed my curious look, he smiled and shrugged.

"When we reach the mountains, it'll cool off a bit."

After we climbed in altitude, the first stop on our *tour* were gun emplacements overlooking the jungles we had just passed through. This was followed by various numbers of defensive positions built to trap an enemy foolish enough to advance in the face of a crossfire of deadly artillery and mortar fire.

Three long hours later, we finally arrived at a sophisticated complex of caves.

A seasoned squad leader who had been acting as our guide pointed toward the caverns. "These caves here in the mountains, and others like it throughout the north of Luzon, can hold thousands of our troops. These emplacements are a formidable obstacle to MacArthur as he moves through the area." He chuckled, then motioned for us to follow.

As the squad of soldiers stood guard outside the cave, we followed the corporal into the dark caverns. It was an immediate relief from the damning heat outside.

I noticed that Yasuda seemed nervous and uneasy, and I asked him why.

"It's nothing," he said nervously, then glanced over his shoulder.

I shrugged off his concern, thinking perhaps he was claustrophobic and silently grateful for the respite from the heat outside.

As we were led deeper into the cavern, the squad leader pointed out the ammunition and supplies stored in anticipation of the siege to come. We were shown each and every cave, clearly meant to demonstrate the preparation of our Army, until we arrived at one cavern that was sealed with metal bars and a padlocked gate.

"What's in there?"

"That's the Command Center," the corporal uttered. "Classified." He then quickly directed us back toward the main entrance.

The humid, sticky air enveloped us once again as the sun beat down on my exposed head. I silently cursed my decision not to bring a hat with me from the hotel.

We all climbed back into the truck for our long journey back to Manila when I heard Yasuda gasp, followed by sounds all too familiar to me.

I watched as Yasuda clutched at his chest, then fell forward. A crimson pool of fresh blood spread on the dirt under his motionless body. I had no time to go to his aid as bullets peppered the ground all around me. I fell flat on the ground, looked for cover, then crawled quickly under the truck.

The piercing *rata-tat-tat* of automatic gunfire hammered the truck above me, and the thud of dead and wounded bodies toppled out of the vehicle like dominoes. Then, landing inches away from my hiding spot, the body of the squad leader thudded into the dirt—his dead eyes wide open and with a look of surprise as they stared back at me.

The brutal surprise attack ended as quickly as it commenced.

I remained motionless, too afraid to crawl from my hiding spot, when I saw a pair of dirty combat boots and camouflaged legs walk towards me.

A soldier squatted down and pointed a rifle at my head. "Get up," a soft voice ordered.

I crawled out from under the truck and was shocked to see an attractive woman pointing an automatic rifle at my chest. Except for the fatigues, she was stylishly dressed for a soldier—hair combed back, wearing bright red lipstick, and her nails impeccably manicured and polished. Behind her, a few other guerrillas stood with their rifles at the ready.

"Who are you?" she said as she circled around me and moved the tip of her rifle around my linen suit.

"I'm a Japanese war correspondent," I stammered.

She motioned to one of the guerrillas to her left, and the soldier stepped forward and grabbed me by the arm. "Move," he growled. He pressed his rifle into my lower back and shoved me toward the jungle.

The Resistance

That night, I found myself a prisoner in the guerrillas' camp somewhere deep in the mountains. I was still struck by the unusual presence of the attractive woman as I watched her talk with her men under a canopy of trees.

"Surprised?" one of her fellow guerrillas asked as he approached. He held a rifle and was rather large for a Filipino.

"Who is she?" I managed to ask.

"Her name is Remedios Gomez-Paraiso. Otherwise known as Commander Liwayway of the Hukbalahap resistance." The large Filipino guerrilla appeared amused by my surprise. "Does that help you?"

I shook my head. "No. I'm not familiar with the Filipino resistance."

"I wouldn't think so," he replied. "Your censored war news would say little of what was *really* going on here the last few years." His upper lip turned tight with disgust. "And I doubt your war reporting included the atrocities committed under Yamashita's command." He poked at my chest with his rifle. "Atrocities too numerous to mention were committed by the Japs on Luzon. In the Batangas Province alone, twenty-five thousand men, women, and children—all unarmed noncombatant civilians—were brutally massacred and exterminated."

As I had no answer for him, I tried to change the subject. "Can you tell me a little more about Liwayway?"

His mood remained as he replied sarcastically, "Why? You want to do a story on her."

"Let's just say that I'm curious. She looks like she's going to a social function."

He shot me a withering look, wondering if I was worth his bother. "She dresses up to show the troops that she is fearless and calm, not afraid to die in combat. She combines her femininity with ferociousness, and that earns our respect."

"She's kind of hard to believe," I said.

"Believe it," he snapped. "She once challenged a comrade to a duel because she felt disrespected by his sexual innuendos."

"I see. And why did she join the resistance?"

"To avenge the murder of her father by the Japanese. He was the vice-mayor of her village. She was only twenty-two years old at the time." He glanced over at Liwayway. "A very enigmatic personality but every inch a woman. She is proud to be a Huk Amazon and we are honored to follow her."

"Giving this reporter my bio, Valmores?" Liwayway said as she approached us.

"A little," he said. "He's very interested in you."

"Maybe you want to do story on me?" she asked.

"I told him," said Valmores, "that whatever he reports back, will never see the light of day."

She leaned over and looked me straight in the eyes. "Well, then. Why shouldn't we kill you?"

"Because... I'm just a war correspondent," I stuttered.

"Or a spy for Yamashita."

"No. That was not my reason to come to the Philippines."

"Why then?"

"Stolen gold," I whispered.

The two exchanged a look before breaking out in laughter. "You mean the stolen gold of the Prince?"

"Prince Chichibu?"

Valmores cocked his head. "Yes. How did you know?" I looked

at both of them before responding. "I've been chasing that stolen gold since Nanking. How do you know about it?"

Liwayway tilted her head towards Valmores. "You're looking at the Prince's valet."

"Please. Tell me. What do you know?"

Off Liwayway's look, Valamores went on to tell me how he had been the personal valet to the Prince and had helped him store large amounts of gold bars and other valuable stolen artifacts in the caves of Luzon.

"Where are they now?" I pressed. "And who else knows?"

Valmores was quiet for some time before responding. "The Prince made sure *no one* would know. One night, dynamite charges were set off in the access tunnels, entombing the engineers, all the Filipino workers, and even his own soldiers once the job was done. He then slipped out by submarine back to Japan."

"And how did you survive?" I asked. "Why didn't he kill you?"

"He said he'd spare me as a reward for my service to him."

"I was told that this treasure was enormous and came from all the conquered territories."

Valmores shook his head. "Not as much as you think. The gold and artifacts were looted only from the Philippines."

"No gold bars from China or Singapore?"

He shook his head once again. "Only Filipino National Bank bars. Bedsides, by 1943, the Japanese were no longer in control of the seas. It didn't make sense to bring in something that valuable here when you know it's going to be lost to the Americans anyway."

I was demoralized and it showed. "Was Unit 731 ever mentioned?"

"Never heard of it," he said, then whispered something to Liwayway.

"If you want," she replied before turning her back on me and walking away.

Valmores shouldered his rifle. "I'm going to return the favor the Prince gave me," he said. "We're letting you go."

Debriefed

"General Yamashita wants to talk to you," an aide to the General said as soon as I reported back to Imperial Army Headquarters.

Before I could even set my bag down, the aide ushered me straight into the General's office. Yamashita stared at me and said, "You're alive. How?"

"I was captured."

"And how did you manage to escape?"

"I didn't. The Filipino guerrillas let me go."

"Why?" Yamashita asked.

"Non-combatant," was my quick reply.

"I see. Lucky for you. Have a seat," Yamashita offered.

I sat down in a chair in front of his desk as Yamashita took a seat as well. "Now tell me, what did you learn about them? Anything that can help us locate this group?"

"No. I was blindfolded and kept in confinement." Although the lie blurted from my lips, part of me was comforted by the fact that it wasn't a complete fabrication—I learned of no tactical information that the Army could use.

"It was quite *noble* of the enemy to let you go," Yamashita said sarcastically.

More noble than the massacres under your command, I wanted to reply, but I wanted to get out of there as soon as possible and back to Japan.

Yamashita scrutinized me for another moment, then must have

come to the conclusion that I was not worthy of any more of his time. "Pick up your travel voucher from the Public Relations Officer." He pointed a finger toward his door, then returned his attention to the paperwork on his desk. "Sayōnara."

Miyoko

I returned to Tokyo in the beginning of October 1944 and immediately recognized that it was a changed city. Due to the gasoline shortage, I boarded a bus that ran on wood. A compartment for burning the wood had been installed on the front side of the bus, opposite the driver. Every time the bus stopped to load and unload passengers, the bus driver would feed more wood into the fuel compartment.

As the bus passed through the city, I noticed that lawns and flower gardens had been turned into mini-vegetable gardens.

After a quick bath at home—a home that seemed so foreign to me as it was seldom used over the past few years—I went to the office.

"I guess you were right," I informed Sakura. "The Army in the Philippines agrees with you. They believe that will be the next target MacArthur will strike."

Sakura chomped on his ever-present cigar. "Tell me something I *don't* know," he replied.

So I told him of the Filipino guerrillas.

"And they simply let you go?"

"Hai. I don't suppose you'd let me write an article about my experience with the guerrillas? You know. Human interest?"

He let out an uproarious laugh.

"I take that as a no."

"Save it for your memoirs. *After* the war." His smile quickly faded from his face. "There's no hiding the military predicament this country is in any longer. Saipan has committed *gyokusai,* and the government is preparing the population for the battles to come. The numbers of soldiers going to the front has dramatically increased, and they're even drafting high school children. It seems as if the home islands are being systematically emptied."

Sakura turned and gazed out his office window and became uncharacteristically quiet. "They're demolishing houses around munitions factories and other important buildings around Tokyo in order to create fire breaks to protect the facilities in the event of air raids. They're preparing the population for what is to come." He returned his gaze back to me. "*That's* your next assignment. Get down to Hiroshima and look up that naval officer's family. Do a piece on how they're preparing."

I nodded and then picked up today's edition on Sakura's desk and scanned the article about the latest government decree. "The government really thinks the population will swallow this tripe? Surrendering all those islands was a deliberate tactic to draw the Americans closer as a ploy so that we can get at them?"

My esteemed editor shrugged his shoulders and once again peered out his window. "You have your assignment."

✳ ✳ ✳

Miyoko Fujiyama sat in her garden dressed in her *monpe*—Japanese-type pantaloons—that made up for its unattractiveness by being very warm and practical against the fall's cold weather.

As she sat there in the early morning dawn, she suddenly felt an itch near her neck. A dragonfly had perched on her shoulder, making no effort to move, even as she turned her head. She noticed the insect's large black eyes staring straight at her, and they appeared moist as if with tears. They reminded her of Yoshi's eyes, and she felt an overwhelming surge of loss. One son dead, and another missing in action.

"Mama-san," came a voice from behind her.

It was her daughter, Suki.

"We have a guest." Suki stepped aside to where I stood with my hands clasped behind my back.

"Kon'nichiwa, dono Fujiyama," I said politely.

"Mr. Koga," she replied. "How nice to see you again." She pointed to the door. "Come inside where it is warm."

As we all moved to the living room, Suki excused herself disappearing somewhere in the house.

"What brings you here?" Miyoko asked.

"Another assignment. I'm doing a story of how the war has affected the average Japanese family."

"I see. And I take it that you want to interview *me*?" she smiled.

"Hai. If you would be so inclined."

"I'd be honored," she said quietly.

After we settled into our seats, I cleared my throat and began yet another interview. "Tell me in your own words," I said. "But first, how is your family?"

"Suki is working at the *Nakajima Aircraft Company* just outside of Tokyo. It's tedious and very sad that so many of our young women have to do such work." She lowered her eyes. "But such are the times."

"And your younger son?"

"Kenji?"

"Yes, Kenji."

Her eyes brightened at the mention of her youngest son. "Kenji is happy and with his friend Black Patch today. The two have become completely inseparable. They're out doing heaven knows what." Then her voice turned somber. "But I fear for him. Many young students are being sent to the front as student draftees to fight this horrible war."

"Yes. I've heard. And Connor? How is he faring in all of this?"

Her mood lightened once again. "Connor is pining away. Is that the correct American term?"

I nodded and smiled. "It seems Connor has been teaching you some English."

"Hai. In any event, he's *pining away* for my sister's daughter. It seems he is in love even though I warned him about forming a relationship with a geisha."

"Oh? She's a geisha?"

"Hai. And a very good one at that."

"What of your eldest son? Hiryo?"

She lowered her head. "He's missing in action. *Erai wa ne.* So brave."

I hated that my interview felt as if I was prying into family matters. "I'm sorry to hear that. I'm sure that he'll be found," I offered, but my words rang hollow. "And what of your husband?"

She attempted a brave smile. "He survived the sea battle around Saipan. That's all I know. He called me from Okinawa and couldn't reveal much due to security reasons. But the tone in his voice expressed a deep sadness. A sense of fatality. I worry for him."

I decided to change the subject. "So tell me. How is your family coping with the war?"

"Oh. How bad of me," she said, quickly standing to her feet. "Let me make you some tea."

And before I could decline the offer, she hurried off into the kitchen.

A few moments later, I heard a scream come from the kitchen. I rushed in and found Miyoko standing in the middle of the room holding a broken pot with tea leaking onto the floor.

"I am so sorry," she cried. "Nothing is good here in Japan anymore. Nothing. Most of our clothes are in tatters and utensils like this are made of cheap material that break so easily."

"That's alright, Miyoko. I didn't want any tea anyway." I bent down to help her clean the liquid off the floor.

"Thank you, Koga-san," she sighed and took my hand in hers. "Let me answer the rest of your questions now."

Once back in the living room, I continued with my interview. "Tell me about the rationing. How has that affected you?"

"Almost everything has become affected," she began. "First it was gasoline and coal. Then sugar... and even matches were rationed.

Finally, it was the rice. Sake is no longer completely made of rice, but from sweet potatoes and acorns. And what little rice we have, I serve with small portions of pickles and dried fish to provide enough food. Shark and whale skin has replaced leather."

She lowered here eyes as her words triggered such sadness. "We had to sell off many of our prized possessions to survive. *Onionskin living*, we have started calling it, because the sale of each prized possession brings tears to our eyes."

"I see," I said, not knowing what I could say that would give her any comfort or hope. I moved on. "How does the rationing system work in the neighborhoods?"

"It's organized by the *tonarigumi*—the neighborhood rationing group. There is a chairman of each association, and it's a rotating position through the head of each household." She stared down at her hands. "With my husband gone, I fill in as the head of our home the best that I can manage. It's a very stressful position having to make allocations based on what we were told by the authorities."

I noticed that her palms had turned yellow. "What is that from? Are you ill?"

She laughed softly. "Hai. We all are. Fruit is very rare. Our district is lucky enough to have many oranges and tangerines. We've eaten so many of them that our palms have stained yellow."

"And how are you coping with such a restricted diet?"

She lowered her voice as if the walls had ears. "Because of my husband's naval duties, we are able to obtain *special rations* from the German Association. That helps. That and the black market, of course."

"Domo arigato, Miyoko," I said, then stood to leave. "You were very helpful."

"Must you leave?" she almost pleaded. "I have so few friendly adults to talk to here."

I could see the desperation and despair etched on her face. I returned to my seat and smiled. "Perhaps I can stay for a little while longer. Why don't we try and make some more tea?"

Black Patch

"How is your *Kinrohoshi* coming?" Kenji asked.

"Not good," Black Patch replied dolefully. "My *Kinrohoshi* was denied. I could not get a doctor's certificate for my exemption to volunteer working in a factory." His attitude turned even gloomier. "And I am *not* going into the Army!" he shouted into the sky.

Kenji put his finger up to his friend's lips. "Shush. Be quiet," he said. "Those are dangerous thoughts. If someone should hear..." He grabbed Black Patch by the hand and pulled him faster. "Come on. We're already late for school."

When they arrived at the school grounds, they were greeted by students carrying and waving small Japanese flags that gathered around a makeshift platform. Standing upon the platform was the principal and a teacher.

"Another grand send-off of a teacher," Black Patch grumbled. "Before too long, they'll be no one left except for old men and children."

"That's Mr. Handa," Kenji mused. "He risked his life saving the portrait of the Emperor during the classroom fire last year."

"Sure. But if he had failed, he would have had to commit suicide," Black Patch snipped.

The principal stepped to a microphone and commenced the send-off ceremony for Mr. Handa. "To give up one's life in defense of our nation is the dearest wish of a man in Japan. It's not a question of victory or defeat, it's a question of how much one will sacrifice in the service of our country!"

Black Patch turned to Kenji. "Enough of this." He grabbed Kenji's arm. "Let's get out of here."

They quietly backed away from the ceremony, hid their school bags behind refuse cans, and quickly left through the east gate.

After getting safely out of earshot, Kenji peered over at his friend. "Well, where are we off to?"

"To the movies," Black Patch replied with a grin.

They boarded a streetcar and headed for the movie district of *Shinkaichi Shingo*.

As they traveled down the street, Kenji elbowed Black Patch. "Let's see an Enoken movie. He always makes funny movies."

"I'd rather see a swashbuckler movie," Black Patch countered. "There's a good one playing now called *Kurama Tengu*."

They argued for few moments until Kenji finally gave in. "Fine. Pirate movie it is."

✷ ✷ ✷

After the movie, Black Patch returned home to find his family gathered in the living room—each of them wearing a grim expression.

"What's the matter? What's going on?" Then he noticed that his parents were clutching a red card in their hands, and he knew instantly why the mood was so bleak.

It was a draft notice.

"We are so sorry," his mother muttered. At her side, his father said nothing, simply stared at the red card in his hand like a death notice.

"I won't go!" Black Patch said defiantly.

"Son. You have no choice," his father said, pulling nervously on his thin mustache. "You must or you will dishonor your family."

"I don't care!" Black Patch screamed and stormed out of the house.

He ran with no particular destination in mind—only that he had to escape.

Finally, out of breath and with tears stinging his eyes, Black Patch's journey ended at the local train station. He stood on the platform on weak knees, his vision blurred by streaks of tears. He walked up and down the platform several times until he heard the familiar sound of an oncoming train.

It was on time, as always, public transit not affected by the war.

As the train sped into the station, Black Patch came to a definitive decision. He walked to the end of the platform, said a silent pray, and to the horror of those around him, simply stepped off the platform and into the on-rushing train.

Amidst the screams of bystanders and shriek of metal against metal, his mangled body was dragged almost a hundred feet before the engineer could bring the train to a final stop.

Perhaps

Miyoko wrapped her arms around her youngest son and rocked him gently. "I'm so sorry to hear the news, Kenji. I know he was a dear friend."

Kenji looked into her eyes with a look of loss and utter confusion—his best friend and cohort was dead. "I don't understand, Mama-san. Why would he kill himself? Black Patch was not a coward."

Miyoko shook her head. "No one could really know for sure." She continued to rock and sooth her son. "Perhaps he was braver than you think. In Japan today, those who disagree with the destructive policies of our country can only prove the courage of their convictions by taking their own life."

Kenji hung his head, and between violent sobs, he managed to say, "Perhaps you are right, Mama-san. Just perhaps."

Grounded

It was a pouring wet night in October of 1944 as Fujiyama made his way to the Okinawa naval hospital. The gloomy weather matched his mood as he pulled his coat collar over his head to ward off the rain, but it did little to keep him dry.

Once in the hospital, he was directed by a nurse to Hiryo's room. "I'm sorry to hear about your ankle and leg," Fujiyama said to his son as he took a seat on the bed.

"They tell me once this cast comes off, you can still train pilots to fly."

Hiryo let out a weary sigh. "Hai. I can still do my duty. I'll be training new recruits at the Kanoya naval base. And you, father?"

"The fleet will be leaving soon for the Philippines to oppose the American landings there." Although not intended, he mimicked his son's sigh. "It will be the last gasp for the IJN. All that's left of the fleet will be sortied for the Philippine defense."

"Do you still have command of your carrier?"

"Hai. The *Zuikaku*. It has been repaired and readied for new action." There was a long pause of reflection before Fujiyama continued. "I have a meeting with Admiral Ugaki, the Naval Chief of Staff. I expect him to give me my orders today."

"Good luck, sir," Hiryo said.

Fujiyama stood and lingered in the room for a moment, searching for a way to depart his son's side without such formality, but failed to do so. So, he simply saluted Hiryo and exited the room.

On the way out of the hospital, Fujiyama ran into Ensign Daiki Onaga—his yeoman on the *Zuikaku*. Onaga gave Fujiyama a sharp salute. "I'm here to see my cousin, sir. How is he doing?"

"Good. But his days of flying combat missions are over."

"A shame, Sir. A real shame."

"Hai," Fujiyama replied. "Will I see you on the *Zuikaku*?"

"No, sir. I've been assigned to the battleship, *Yamato*," Onaga responded. The Ensign then smiled as if embarrassed. "I wanted to thank you, Sir. For taking me under your wing, so to speak."

"Happy to do it," Fujiyama replied. "The *Yamato* is a good ship. Take good care of her. And good luck to you, son."

Sacrificed

"Captain Fujiyama to see Admiral Ugaki."

The staff sergeant snapped to his feet and saluted. "Have a seat, sir. The Admiral will be right with you."

Fujiyama noted the change of seating in the Admiral's outer office. In Yamamoto's time, it had been appointed with fashionable furniture designed for the comfort of visiting dignitaries. But the needs of the war necessitated a more utilitarian downsizing of everything these days.

Fujiyama wasn't seated long before Ugaki came out of his office. "Nice to see you again, my friend," Ugaki offered with a genuine tone. "I'm happy you survived the battle."

"Thank you, sir." Fujiyama gave the Admiral a salute. "But many of my pilots did not."

"Too many, I'm afraid," he sighed. Ugaki then glanced at the staff sergeant before returning his attention back on Fujiyama. "Come into my office. We need to talk."

Fujiyama took a seat opposite Ugaki's desk and watched as the Admiral shuffled some papers off to the side.

"You are probably aware of what's happening in the Philippines, correct?" Ugaki asked.

Fujiyama nodded. "When do you expect the American's to invade?"

"Very soon. At Leyte." He pulled a sheet of paper from the pile on his desk. "This is a summary of the naval defense of the Philippines. I'd like you to take a moment and review it."

Fujiyama accepted the official looking report and carefully read it over. After a few minutes he said, "Three forces?"

"Hai. A Northern Force, a Central Force, and a two-part Southern Force. It's called Operation Sho-Go 1. All three forces converging on Leyte to repel the coming American invasion there. We've committed almost the entire surface fleet to the conflict. The *Yamato,* along with four other battleships, and an assortment of cruisers and destroyers under the command of Vice Admiral Takeo Kurita, make up the Central Force. It's to proceed through the San Bernardino Strait, sail down the coast of Samar, and fall on the American invasion fleet from the northeast."

"And what of the other forces?"

"Rear Admiral Nishimura will lead the Southern Force that consists of additional battleships and warships through the Surigao Strait, just south of Leyte." He tapped at the report in Fujiyama's hands. "And Admiral Jisaburo Ozawa will command the Northern Force. He will use your carrier as his flagship. In addition to your carrier, the Northern Force will consist of three light carriers, two battleships, three light cruisers, and eight destroyers."

Fujiyama nodded. "Hai. That will give the Americans something formidable to deal with. And when will I receive my contingent of planes?"

Ugaki sat back in his chair and sighed. "Outside of a few search planes, you won't."

Fujiyama was speechless for a moment. "With all due respect, sir, what are carriers without planes?"

There was a heavy lull of silence in the room before the Admiral answered with a single word. "Bait."

Fujiyama couldn't believe his ears. He knew what that meant. "The ships will be helpless against U.S. carrier planes. Completely defenseless."

Ugaki nodded his agreement. "The Northern Force will decoy the American naval forces away from the invasion beaches, and if absolutely necessary, be sacrificed. The four aircraft carriers will prove to be irresistible to the Americans. Besides, we have few attack planes to give the carriers. As you are aware, most of them are at the bottom of the Philippine Sea."

The two men were quiet for a while, then Ugaki stood up, walked over to Fujiyama and placed his hand on his shoulder. "I'm sorry, my friend."

With a heavy heart, Fujiyama stood, saluted the Admiral, and left the office.

On his way out of naval headquarters, Fujiyama passed by stirring pictures of aircraft carriers, battleships, and cruisers of a once proud Imperial Navy. Many of these ships were merely ghosts now ,and others would soon join them. Ships whose only purpose now was to be sacrificed.

How did we come to such a fate? Fujiyama thought as he stepped outside into a fierce rainstorm.

The Yamato

Daiki peered out over the choppy, gray waters from the helm of the giant battleship *Yamato* as it steamed towards the Philippines.

"First time behind the helm?" asked the executive officer, Commander Hoshimoto. "Nervous?"

"A little. I must admit," Daiki replied. "I was just a yeoman on the *Zuikaku*."

"And the *Yamato* is much bigger," Hoshimoto replied proudly, and a fast beast at that." He pointed to a large battleship off their port beam. "This and her sister ship, the *Musashi*, are the heaviest and most powerfully armed battleships ever constructed. But don't you worry. If Fujiyama recommended you for this assignment, you must have had a very good record."

Daiki nodded, then looked out over the horizon. "Do you think we'll see any typhoons, sir?"

"October is the season for it." He patted Daiki on the back. "But it'll take quite a storm to overcome this ship. What you need to worry about is the other storm. The Americans."

Lone Survivor

Fujiyama stared out over the bridge at the black, billowing clouds on the horizon as the Northern Force approached Cape Engano, located at the very northern tip of the island of Luzon. It was typhoon weather, and a troubling thought kept racing through his mind.

Admiral Ozawa, who stood near Fujiyama, noticed his pensive expression. "What bothers you, Captain?"

Fujiyama kept his gaze out upon the sea. "I was thinking of a typhoon."

"Divine Wind? Like the one that destroyed and saved Japan from two Mongol fleets under Kublai Khan?"

Fujiyama finally turned to face the Northern Force Commander-in-Chief. "No, sir. I was thinking of the *Fourth Fleet Incident.*"

"Oi," Ozawa grunted. "The typhoon of '35."

"Hai. It inflicted extensive damage to our ships during those fleet exercises."

The Admiral placed his hand on Fujiyama's shoulder. "That type of storm damage *cannot* occur with this ship." He thumped his hand on the steel railing before him to accentuate his remark. "I wouldn't be concerned with that threat, Captain. To her credit, the *Zuikaku* is the most successful Japanese aircraft carrier of the war. She alone sank the British ships *Hermes, Cornwall,* and *Dorsetshire.* Her planes sunk the *USS Lexington* and severely damaged the *Yorktown* at Coral Sea. In the battles around Guadalcanal, she was the bane of the *USS Enterprise's* existence, damaging her twice, plus crippling the *Hornet* that ultimately led to her demise. She is a proud ship and will do her duty. I promise you that."

Fujiyama knew the pedigree of his ship well. But he also knew that the *Zuikaku* happened to be the last surviving fleet carrier that attacked Pearl Harbor. Knowing that, the U.S. Navy would be gunning for her, and she had no fighters to defend herself with.

Ozawa checked his watch. "When do you expect our search planes to return?"

Fujiyama looked out on the horizon. "Soon, sir. I... Oi," he noted. "I see one now. But..."

It dawned on both Fujiyama and Ozawa at the same time as the lookout on the bridge cried, "Enemy plane!"

"We've been spotted. Sound general quarters," Fujiyama said, then more like a prayer, added, "Let's hope our search planes have as much luck."

Devastation

They did indeed.

A search plane found the American Fleet in late afternoon, and Ozawa ordered all the remaining aircraft of the four carriers to unleash an attack on the Americans.

The result proved to be devastating, but not to the Americans.

Not a single Japanese plane returned to the carriers. They were decimated by the defenses of the American fleet, and the few that survived the attack, made their way to airfields on Luzon.

Now it was the U.S. Navy's turn. Wave after wave of American fighters, bombers, and torpedo planes fell upon the Japanese Force.

"The *Chitose* is sinking!" the yeoman who stood next to Fujiyama and Ozawa cried.

"Evasive maneuvers!" Fujiyama barked.

But it was to no avail. With a devastating thud that shook the ship to its very core, a torpedo slammed into the side of the *Zuikaku*, almost knocking Ozawa to the deck.

Fujiyama caught the Admiral by the arm, and they reached for the railing on bridge to steady themselves.

"My God... they're all over us," Fujiyama exclaimed as he glanced skyward toward fifty-plus U.S. naval bombers and torpedo planes swarming all around the crippled carrier.

Bombs rained down on the *Zuikaku* with nine proving to be direct hits. Gunners from forward and aft anti-aircraft stations flew fifteen feet into the air as bombs from above exploded near their stations. Crewmen that weren't instantly killed, dragged themselves back to their anti-aircraft gun to take on the next planes.

"Lower my flag," Ozawa said bitterly. "I'm transferring my command to the cruiser *Oyodo.*"

Fujiyama reluctantly gave the order to abandon ship. The crew gathered on the aft deck of the carrier, saluted the bridge, then made for the lifeboats as the *Zuikaku* listed heavily to starboard.

Fujiyama shook his head in hopelessness as he watched dozens of sailors floating dead on the surface of the ocean, while the survivors swam over their fallen comrade's bodies and hauled themselves onto lifeboats.

As Fujiyama watched the madness of scrambling seamen abandoning his ship, another horror appeared before his eyes-the distinct wake of several torpedoes headed straight toward his crippled carrier. Fujiyama reached for a guardrail as a heavy thump, then another and another, slammed into *Zuikaku's* sides.

The doomed carrier shuttered violently as the forward lift collapsed into the hanger deck, carrying fleeing sailors with it, and into a cauldron of fire below decks.

Plumes of dark smoke belched from the *Zuikaku,* marking its destiny of disaster with the others in the fleet. All four carriers, the battleship *Ise,* and two destroyers were now ablaze and on their way to the depths below.

"Sir," the yeoman implored. "You have to abandon ship."

The overwhelming thought of going down with his command raced through in his mind, but then Fujiyama remembered his wife and children. He couldn't leave them without a husband and father.

Ocean water washed over the end of the flight deck as the crippled *Zuikaku* began to sink stern first. The yeoman pulled Fujiyama with him and exited the bridge.

But the condemned carrier had reached the point of instability and she began to roll over on her side.

Fujiyama reached up over his head to grab onto whatever he could, but as he did so, the superstructure of the ship above came crashing down upon him. The yeoman let out a terrified scream as the heavy, smoldering metal fell upon him and Fujiyama, crushing the two men under tons of unforgiving iron and steel.

Fujiyama's death was mercifully short as the *Zuikaku* rolled over and sank deeper and deeper into sea.

A Terrible Vision

I left my editor's office and emerged into a cold, harsh November day. While waiting for a cab on this clear, crisp morning, my eyes drifted towards Mt. Fuji in the distance, and noticed white billowy clouds silently advancing up the treacherous slopes.

As I stood in the bitter chill, I could still hear my editor's words ringing in my ears. *Tojo has resigned, and Army General Kuniaki Koiso has been appointed Prime Minister and formed a new Cabinet. Our readers want to know what the government does next. Especially their response to the American conquest of the Philippines. It's an event that is impossible even for the Thought Police to hide from the public. I want you to talk to Hiyakawa and find out what Japan is in for.*

When I arrived at Hiyakawa's home, he led me to his study and took no time in guessing the purpose of my visit. "I assume this is not a social call," he said in his gentle voice while guiding me to chair.

We sat quietly for a few moments as I observed the lonely emptiness of his home. "I miss our chats with your wife," I said softly. "I'm so sorry."

"Domo arigato."

"Are you handling it well?"

He lowered his eyes. "As well as can be expected. I spend most of my time at the Buddhist Temple. It comforts me."

Although I hated to pry upon his misery, I wanted to know his real thoughts.

"I'm sorry to have to ask this, but do you think Colonel Sato killed your wife?"

"Oi. It wasn't the Kempeitai. They put Barbara in prison to intimidate me... to keep me in line. What happened was not of their making." For the first time, I saw him stiffen his jaw in determination—unlike someone of such a mild disposition. "But I am free of them now. Now that Barbara is dead."

I know what he meant. Sato and his ilk could no longer intimidate him. I decided to change the subject to something less painful. "Tell me, your Excellency. Where does Japan stand now?"

He wasted no words. "Leyte Gulf was a complete and utter disaster. The Imperial Japanese Fleet ceases to exist as an effective fighting force. Except for our land-based planes, America has the undisputed command of the sea. There is no further use assigned to our surface vessels, with the exception of some special ships."

He took a long, painful breath. "Imperial Headquarters has become incapable of any effective response. Time and again commanders fought their own island battles with little or no help in the form of actual reinforcements, or any kind of coordinated strategy from Tokyo. Even causing innocent civilians to die along with them in their island strongholds. And the destructive power of the American submarines has a stranglehold on Japan. Less and less food, oil, and raw materials make it to Japan's harbors everyday."

"And the militarists. Have they changed their tune, now?"

"They no longer believe that Japan can prevail on the battlefield."

"So, they're talking of surrender," I said matter-of-factly.

Hiyakawa shook his head. "No. Most of the War Cabinet believes that Japan could not be forced to surrender. But when they see that there is no longer any escape and contemplate the punishments Japan will surely endure, they will continue the war simply because there is no other choice."

He shifted his weight in his chair. "The prevailing strategy now is to make every American offensive as costly as possible, and simply hope and pray that we outlast the Americans."

"Madness," I scoffed.

"There's even more," he said cryptically. "But, I'm sorry. Can I make you some tea?"

"Hai. That would be nice."

Several minutes later, while I turned over in my mind the cryptic statement he left me with, he returned from the kitchen with two porcelain cups and pot of green tea.

He poured us both a cup then sat back in his chair. "Do you know the meaning of *Gyokusai?*"

"Yes. *Better to be a gem smashed to bits than a whole tile.* Our newspaper first used the term in April of '43, when it reported the fate of our troops defending Attu Island in the Aleutians."

Hiyakawa nodded. "Gyokusai is an ancient Chinese classic, but now it is being used to mean *total annihilation.*"

"You mentioned something more than madness."

Hiyakawa placed his teacup on the small table in front of him. "*Kamikaze.* Suicide attacks. Divine Wind. The first *deliberate* attacks of the war were at Leyte Gulf."

I was completely stunned. "That was not reported to the press."

"And there will be more. Admiral Ugaki made the case for a Special Attack Force to be used against the American Fleet at the last War Cabinet meeting."

"Was it approved?"

"Hai. Recruitment and training programs have already been established." He sat back in his chair and closed his eyes as if in contemplation. "Ours is a country in which every person lacks any kind of individuality. We submit to our leader's will and simply do what we are told. We have fought this war right up to the present, all the while saying 'We will win! We will win!' while events have proven our delusions otherwise."

Hiyakawa reopened his eyes, then hung his head. "The American bombers will now come. After that, millions of Japanese will die in a national suicide pact." He hung his head. "I will not lie. It is my misfortune to have been born a Japanese."

We both were quiet for some time, each with our own tortured thoughts. Finally, I asked the question that haunted me on a daily basis. "How will all of this end?"

Hiyakawa looked up with an odd expression on his face. "There is a Buddhist monk at my temple. One evening after meditation, he told us of a vision he had—really, a prediction. About a weapon, so powerful, that it could destroy an entire city all at once. A weapon so fierce, it would change the course of history and create an era of fear of the total destruction of civilization."

I stared at Hiyakawa and waited to see if he was joking. Jesting appeared to be the last thing on his mind.

"The monk had to be mad," I replied.

"He was deadly serious," Hiyakawa responded.

"And what will you do?" I asked.

"I have nothing to lose now. I will work with the Peace Faction in the Diet and hope we can end this madness before millions of Japanese die."

Preparing for the Worst

"Connor, Kenji," Miyoko implored, "Please cover the lamps in the house. Your sister is not here, and I need your help."

At night, civilians were prohibited from brightly lit rooms. If a household happened to forget, air raid wardens who were responsible for checking on the blackout would pound loudly on windows or doors to complain.

Kenji was even instructed not to listen to his music.

"Kutabare!" Kenji scoffed. "They can go to hell. As if the American bombers could look down, listen, and find me."

But there was something about the darkened streets and homes that made people speak in hushed whispers, and the so-called *family shelters* that had been dug in the side yard were no more than a deep hole—exposed, filthy, and damp to boot.

Neighborhood association flyers implored residents to rid their homes of every scrap of metal for weapons for the war effort. Even Kenji's toy metal planes had been sacrificed much to the ire of the young boy.

After Connor and Kenji had covered all the lamps in their home, Miyoko instructed them to report to the neighborhood warden. "The sand bags for putting out fires need to be filled and stacked outside each dwelling along with pails of water. And post our list of air raid materials and equipment on the back door for the inspectors before you leave."

The two boys complied, picked up a broom that looked like a

large fly swatter to beat out flames, and took off into the night. As the boys passed by the side of the house, Connor eyed the long, sharpened bamboo poles that leaned against the sidewall and shook his head. Each member of a household—every man, woman and child over fifteen—was ordered to have and use these makeshift weapons against the invading Americans when they finally stormed the shores.

Air raid preparations and drills weren't the only thing that had changed in the last year. The blockade of the home islands by the American Navy and the constant submarine attacks on Japanese shipping were taking an even greater toll on food supplies which had become even scarcer than before. There was no flour now, and rice was used in almost every dish.

Many of the traditional festivals so revered by the Japanese were indefinitely canceled. The people had no heart left in them. The populace seemed fatigued and exhausted.

Connor wanted no more of these depressing times. He longed for the company of Aiko. He wished he was with Suki in Tokyo but Miyoko—all alone now and with no news from her husband implored the American teenager to stay with her. Despite desperately wanting to be out of the house in the worse kind of way, Connor honored the desire of his Japanese mother and remained at her side.

The Shrill Sound of Fear

Since July of 1944, Suki had been working on an assembly line at the Musashino plant of the Nakajima Aircraft Company just outside Tokyo. Many of her friends wanted no part of the war work and were frightened by the routine air raid drills in their hometown, as well as the frequent warnings of American bombers appearing over the skies of Japan at any given time.

Most of Suki's girlfriends decided to marry farmers due to the safety of the mountains and the food they could provide their families. But Suki wasn't ready for marriage. Not even to Takahashi, who constantly harangued her to marry him every time he returned on leave.

When Suki wrote home detailing her work in the factory, she spoke of how geishas were drafted to provide services in the factory, and how the workers reveled in the smell of fragrant cosmetics for the first time in their lives.

"Very good, Fujiyama," her supervisor would say as he watched her cut pipes into little pieces, then used the machine at her station to make threads on the metal to screw into other pieces. She had no idea what they did, only that they were parts to be used in airplane engines.

"There's talk of you becoming a supervisor," he had informed her one day. "And I agree."

After Suki completed yet another group of piping, she loaded them into a crate.

"Done already?" asked Mitsui, an old man in his late sixties. The burden of the war and the work he produced could be seen in his weary eyes and sat upon his shoulders like a dead weight. Mitsui reached for her crate to load it onto a three-wheeled iron cart with others.

"Can I help you move the carts?" Suki asked.

"Domo," he replied with a smile. "Domo arigato." Because of his thin frame, it was difficult for him to get proper footing, so Suki helped him when she could.

Suki liked the old man because he treated her like his own daughter, saving his bits of sweet cake for her that workers received at lunch. He would often say about his toil, "Sad days. The routine of once happy times are denied, and we are forced to go against the natural feelings we had about family, beauty, truth, and goodness."

Suki knew what he meant. She had seen enough of what the war had done to her family and her country in the hospital where she had once volunteered and in the downtrodden faces of people on the streets.

In unison, the two shoved the iron cart of crates outside of the factory to a large field and dumped them into one of many shallow pits dug into the ground. The pit would be later covered with straw and then dirt to hide the crates from enemy planes.

On their way back to the factory, the single shrill blast of the air raid siren startled them out of their thoughts. They hesitated a moment as the long wail increased to a crescendo, then hung in the air, covering the entire city like a blanket.

It was a horrible sound to Suki. It was as if the city itself was crying out in distress.

"Probably just another high altitude B-29 reconnaissance mission," Mitsui noted.

Normally, a single blast of the siren would not cause any concern, but that reality quickly changed. Just as they reached the backdoor of the factory, they heard anti-aircraft shells burst high in the air above them, leaving behind black and white puffs of smoke.

Mitsui stopped in his tracks and peered towards the sky. "I don't think..." But another siren sounded, cutting off his words. The siren's undulating tone of hoots went up and down, on and on, and piercing the morning air.

Mitsui pointed into the sky as a formation of B-29s appeared over the city. "This is no reconnaissance mission."

Suki quickly grabbed the old man by the arm. "Come. We must get to the shelter."

With Mitsui in tow, Suki hurried towards the air raid shelter that was nothing more than a large, dirt trench.

Suki and Mitsui rushed into a five-foot wide, forty-foot long covered trench where over fifty other factory workers huddled upon the ground.

Over the lip of the shelter, they heard the crackling of anti-aircraft fire, followed by booming sounds that seemed to march in cadence directly towards them.

"They're getting closer," Suki whispered.

Mitsui said nothing. He merely placed his arm around her shoulders and stood in silence.

Explosions shook the ground below their feet, followed by more booming sounds. Frightened murmurs and the sobs of women filled the shelter as the earth rumbled. With each explosion, dirt rained down on top of them.

Then a deafening blast, much louder than the others, echoed through the shelter. "I think they hit the factory," Mitsui said.

The old man dropped his arm from around Suki and headed to the shelter entrance—entranced by the planes overhead and wanting to see the destruction of the factory for himself.

"Wait!" Suki screamed.

But the old man ignored her pleas and disappeared from the shelter curious to see the damage.

Suki pushed past the hordes of other factory workers and stumbled out of the safety of the covered trench. She spotted Mitsui in the middle of the factory yard, scanning the skies above him.

"Look!" He pointed to dark bellowing clouds and towering flames that were consuming the factory.

Mitsui looked to the young woman and shook his head. "I'm afraid this is only the beginning. This will end the mockery of the government's unending tales of victory, he shouted with disdain."

Suki could only shake her head in disbelief as she watched a large section of the factory slowly burn to the ground.

Suki was sent home to Hiroshima while repairs were made at the factory. The moment she walked through the door, she spotted her mother and Kenji huddled on the floor, sobbing. Connor stood above them holding an official-looking notice in his hand.

Miyoko looked into Suki's questioning eyes. "He's dead. Your father is dead."

Suki knelt down with her mother and brother and comforted them while quietly shedding tears of her own.

Her eyes went up to Connor. She wanted to comfort him, too, expecting his eyes to be filled with tears. She was surprised to see just a stoic expression etched upon his face. And in contrast to his dull expression, his eyes were filled with turmoil—and something else. She had no way of knowing that it was a silent vow for justice.

- IN THE EYE OF THE STORM -

1945

A Fateful Call

I stared out the window of my newly assigned office on a cold, blustery day in January of 1945—a day that would irrevocably change my life. The office was tiny and had little to no interior design, but it was *mine*. I had earned this private workspace from Sakura for the fine work done as the newspaper's lead foreign correspondent, even though much of the news of the war I reported was unprintable.

"Call for you," growled Sakura through the paper-thin wall that separated our offices. "If it's personal, keep it brief," he added.

I picked up the phone and answered, "Koga speaking."

"Mr. Koga," a soft voice on the other end of the line replied, "My name is Monsignor Sheehan."

Before I could reply, Monsignor Sheehan continued on. "I ask that you please come to the headquarters of the Catholic Mission here in Tokyo at your earliest convenience. It's very important. Good day." And he hung up.

"Hello? Hello?" I stammered, but the line was nothing but a dial tone.

Now what is that all about? I thought. *But if it's news to cover, perhaps there's a story in the mysterious phone call.*

I called for a cab and made my way downstairs to the front of the building, and to my delight, it was actually snowing. Not a rarity for Tokyo, but I always enjoyed the effects that a gentle snow had on the city, especially in times like these.

I bundled up my coat collar and waited for my cab to appear. It was cold, and I hoped my conveyance would arrive in short order.

It didn't.

I realized that though snow in Tokyo was not unusual, it was infrequent enough that driving in the wet and icy conditions posed a challenge to the average Japanese driver.

My cab finally arrived twenty minutes later, and I was swept away toward my destination. Upon arriving at the Catholic Mission, I entered the reception hall and greeted a young priest sitting behind a small wood carved desk.

"Good afternoon. I am Mr. Koga. I was called here by Monsignor Sheehan."

"Ah. Yes," he replied and opened his desk draw. He handed me an envelope marked *Personal. For Mr. Koga.*

I thanked the priest and found a seat in the hall. I wondered what it was all about as I fingered open the envelope and was surprised at its contents—a most wanted surprise.

The note was short and to the point:

Mr. Koga. I have what you have been looking for. See me as soon as possible.

Father Marquette.'

My thoughts went to the time I met Father Marquette at the French Catholic mission in Manchuria. And although this revelation was well received, it posed a difficult problem—there was no way Sakura would allow me to go to Manchuria as a reporter. If I tried without his approval, I would possess no credentials that would enable me to pass me through security. And since the carrier Zuikaku was reported lost and Fujiyama was at best, missing, the military option was closed to me.

As I racked my brain for ideas, the solution dawned on me like a bolt of lightening. I raced out of the mission, hailed a cab, and was soon on my way to the Palace.

Tennozan

"Yoshihara, my old friend!" Hiyakawa greeted me. Although it was a cordial greeting, I noticed the worry lines that burdened his drawn face. I could only guess that things at the Palace had gone from bad to worse.

Hiyakawa could see the concern in my eyes. "Am I that transparent?"

"Hai. How bad is it?"

"Well, the Emperor is aghast at how the war has turned against Japan. The military was not forthright with the Emperor on attacking America. They had gambled and lost."

"And? What is he to do?"

"The Emperor just consulted with all the Prime Ministers. Nearly every one of them counseled him that Japan has no alternative but to continue the war. The only exception was Prince Fumimaro Konoe, who was also the holdout against the attack on Pearl Harbor. He counseled making peace with the Americans. But, as we all know, he was blatantly ignored."

"What of Kido? Lord Keeper of the Privy Seal?"

Hiyakawa rubbed at his weary face. "He feared that if he became involved in divisive conflicts over national policy, this would undermine the transcendental authority of the Imperial House and the principle of ministerial responsibility."

Hiyakawa waited for a group of passing diplomats to exit the Palace doors before continuing. "The Emperor's ministers have tried to keep him *above the clouds* of political conflict, withholding key information over the years." He clenched his hands into fists at his sides. "I once overhead former Prime Minister Saionji Kinmochi say, *It is not necessary to lie, but tell the Emperor things that will please him, in order to ease his mind.*"

"So what did the Emperor do?"

Hiyakawa sighed in resignation. "He ordered that Japan would fight a final decisive battle. A *tennozan*—a great victory. Not so much to defeat the Americans, but to bleed them in order to secure better peace terms. This, he hoped, might prevent an invasion and occupation of the home islands."

"And what's going to be the *final battle*?" I asked with great anticipation.

Hiyakawa was quiet for a moment before responding. "All things point to Okinawa. The Americans will need to occupy that particular island in order to mount an invasion of Japan."

"How have we come to this, Hiyakawa?" I replied angrily. "How could the Emperor let himself lose control of his country?"

Hiyakawa shook his head, silently wishing he had better answers. "Hirohito endeavored behind the scenes at court to exert his Imperial influence to prevent war. But in every case, Hirohito's informal interventions were to no avail."

"But he is the Emperor, is he not?"

Hiyakawa sighed. "Hirohito was never equipped to deal with the harsh realities of Japanese politics. Instead of order, conflict prevailed all around him. Conflict within the cabinet that changed with alarming frequency and severity. Conflict between the civil and military branches of government, and conflict between the Army and Navy over national defense priorities in foreign policy."

Hiyakawa finally bowed and shook his head. "By interfering in political affairs, both services, especially the Army, concealed its intentions from the Emperor and often acted unilaterally, in total defiance of the government, ultimately making a mockery of the Emperor's influence. And to make matters worse, not only was the Emperor's enigmatic silence often interpreted as signifying his approval of policies leading to war, but he and his advisors feared that any political conflict might trigger another attempted military coup like the February 26th Incident. The Emperor was dictated by the fear of being replaced on the throne by his brother, Prince Chichibu, whose greater sympathies with the Army were well-known."

He looked me straight in the eye, and the makings of a sneer crossed his lips—something I've never seen Hiyakawa reveal. "Do I have to mention the Kwantung Army in Manchukuo?"

I nodded. I knew exactly what Hiyakawa meant. It was doubtful that the supreme command had any real influence over the Kwantung Army. It was feared that the Kwantung Army would not be loyal to the Emperor.

We were both silent until Hiyakawa caught himself and asked, "I'm sorry to bend your ear, old friend. You asked to see me?"

"Hai. I need a favor."

It Was Time

A heavy frost from the night before covered the trees in Miyoko's garden causing the limbs and leaves to bow towards the ground. The weight of this burden expressed her despondent mood, and not even the beautiful blanket of snow that covered much of the country helped elevate her disposition.

The sun—strong and brimming with hope, shining through the chilly sky—revealed foreboding threats by providing a canvas for the contrails of the high flying B-29s that now crisscrossed over the county at will.

Just the day before, a large formation of B-29s flew over the Prefecture on their way to a raid. It was reported that three cities were seriously bombed that day.

"Look, Mama-san!" Kenji cried as the persistent wail of the air raid sirens filled the air. He pointed to the formation of planes glistening like silver reflections high above in the sunlight.

"This is the beginning of the end," Miyoko murmured as puffs of anti-aircraft fire trailed the advancing planes. The raids on cities were getting worse, yet the government fabricated the most outrageous lies of the glorious defense of the country.

Even the presumed comparative safety of night or rainy days were of no comfort. Some of the worst raids came in bad weather. The planes would strike at all hours, and people were afraid to go into the streets.

Miyoko was not alone in her silent dread. Connor's anxiety

increased during these months, and he feared for Aiko's safety in Tokyo. That morning he decided it was time.

"Mama-san," he implored, "I want to visit Suki where she works near Tokyo."

Miyoko knew the real reason for his request. She could see the loneliness in his eyes, and though she feared for his safety outside their home, she could not keep him sheltered forever. At least Suki was there and could help keep him safe.

"Hai," she replied. "Go to her. But Connor-san, please leave when it's dark. Better to travel at night."

"Domo, Mama-san," he replied happily and immediately raced to his room to start packing.

We Are Alone

Connor arrived at the main Tokyo train station later that night. He pulled his heavy coat up over his neck as protection against the cold chill—and recognition.

"*Konnichiwa*, Connor," a voice that he hadn't heard in over a year whispered from behind him.

He turned around to find Jiro standing there. "Jiro!" Connor replied. "What are you doing here?"

"Looking for you."

"Really? And how did you manage to find me?"

"Spoke to your mama-san." Jiro smiled. "She told me about you and the geisha."

Connor's mood soured even more. "What do you want?"

"Some of the young Yakuza are joining a new military organization, a special attack force and they're looking for pilots."

"*You're* not a pilot."

"I soon will be. They'll train me." Jiro placed his hand on Connor's shoulder. "I thought you wanted to be a real Japanese…"

"Not interested. I have to go." And he pushed past Jiro and disappeared from the station, refusing to look back.

He left the Tokyo terminal, hustled down darkened streets empty of citizens, and followed the route shown to him by Aiko, where he finally arrived at her home just before dawn.

"Connor-san!" Aiko cried with joy the moment she opened the door and threw herself into his arms.

Connor held her tight and gave her a long kiss. "I've missed you so much."

She nodded in agreement, then gently took his hand and led him into the kitchen. "Mama-san," she chirped. "Look who's here!"

Mai turned, and a broad smile took over her round face. "So good to see you, Connor-san. You are always welcomed here." Mai then turned to Aiko and seemed to speak without using words.

"Matsumuro is away on business," Aiko replied with a quick dismissal. She turned back to Connor, and with a sparkle in her eye, said, "No need to worry, Connor. We are alone."

Return to Nanking

I arrived in Nanking under a diplomatic passport, courtesy of Hiyakawa. He felt it best—and I agreed—that I enter the mainland through China and away from the direct eyes of the Kwantung Army. I would then make my way to Manchukuo by land. It would be a long and tedious journey, but a discreet one.

But how best to do it?

Then I remembered John Rabe. If he was still in Nanking, maybe he could help.

I flagged down a cycle rickshaw and traveled to the German embassy through bustling streets. It was if the tragedy that was Nanking had never happened. It seemed to be business as usual. The only remnants of war were the number of demolished and damaged buildings I saw en route.

My rickshaw finally pulled up to the entrance of a stone, three-story building that boldly displayed the red and white swastika flag. I handed the driver a few yen and made my way toward the building.

Stationed on both sides of the door were two Wehrmacht uniformed soldiers who scrutinized me with suspicious eyes. *Perhaps Japanese citizens are not frequent visitors to the embassy*, I thought. I flashed my diplomatic passport, and they merely pointed me in the direction of the office.

Behind a small desk perched an elderly German man who I guessed to be the receptionist. "May I help you," he asked in a short, gruff German accent.

"My name is Mr. Koga, and I would like to locate Herr John Rabe."

He raised an eyebrow at the mention of Rabe's name and quickly picked up his phone. "A Mr. Koga here to see Herr Rabe." A beat later he said, "Ja," and hung up. "Someone will be down to see you. Have a seat there."

I complied and waited. And waited. And waited.

About twenty minutes later, a slim young man with short, cropped blond hair bustled through the door. "You are looking for Herr Rabe?"

I nodded. "My name is Yoshihara Koga. Do you know where he might be?"

Instead of a direct answer, the young man simply stated, "Come with me."

As I followed him upstairs, he finally introduced himself. "I am Hans Bauer. I was Herr Rabe's assistant.

"Was?"

"Ja. He left Nanking in the spring of '38 to present Hitler with a letter and show him his report on the invasion of Nanking. He hoped Der Führer would intercede for the Chinese." He saw the surprise in my eyes. "Let's talk in private."

We entered a small anteroom and seated ourselves in two over-stuffed chairs. "Would you like some coffee?" Bauer offered.

I jumped at the chance. "Yes. Please." I hadn't had European coffee—or good coffee of any kind—for many years.

He retrieved a coffee pot and two large cups from the table in front of us and poured the caffeine brew.

I took a pleasurable sip and asked, "What happened to Herr Rabe? Did Hitler act on his report?"

Bauer shook his head. "He was detained and interrogated by the Gestapo, and his letter was never delivered to Hitler. If it weren't for the intervention of his company, Siemens AG, he would have been jailed for sure. For his safety, Siemens posted him at their plant in Afghanistan, and that's where he still is to this day."

He took a long drink of his coffee. "Herr Rabe spoke of you, Mr. Koga. You're a newspaper reporter and were doing a story on the invasion of Nanking. Is that what you are doing now?"

Not knowing or trusting this man, I wasn't prepared to tell him the real reason for my trip. "I'm doing a follow up report for the Foreign Affairs Minister on both China and Manchukuo. Thus the diplomatic passport."

"I see. So how would Mr. Rabe have helped in this matter?"

"By helping me to travel to Manchukuo. I assumed he would know a way either through his company or your embassy."

"Ja. Perhaps we can help you," he replied. "We have a diplomatic flight that leaves for Manchukuo twice a month. The next one is in ten days. You may take that flight if you wish."

And with that, Hans Bauer excused himself, and our coffee chat was over.

Déjà Vu

While waiting for my flight, I found myself spending much of my time around the German embassy. Not that I particularly found the company of Nazis to my liking, but I rather enjoyed the European food served in their embassy cafeteria. It was a far cry from the ration of dried fish and rice that had become my daily diet in Japan.

And being a reporter, I discovered the conversations with the embassy staff served as a window into what was happening to the Axis powers. As the war dragged on, news on that front became less and less a reflection of reality in Japan.

"I heard that the big winter offensive in December of last year didn't go so well," I ventured to ask Bauer one day while we both sipped coffee. "What is Germany to do now?"

He bristled at my remark but came back with a reply that appeared automatic and well-rehearsed. "Trust me, Germany is far from defeated. The Führer says we will soon have a weapon far deadlier than the V1 and V2 rockets—a weapon so powerful that it will destroy an entire city in a single flash. A weapon that will bring about the total destruction of our enemy's civilization."

My skin crawled. Those were almost the exact words of Hiyakawa's Buddhist monk.

Bauer noticed the expression on my face and favored my discomfort with a smile. "Just wait, my Axis friend. This war is far from over."

Beginning of the End

As the awareness in Japan of losing the war increased and the invasion of the home islands loomed over the horizon, the nation prepared itself for the final act of the war.

Air raid drills were now all too frequent, and buildings that had once been white, now stood as black tombstones throughout the cities to make them less visible to air raids.

Bamboo spear drills for Kenji and his fellow students to defend their community against the coming invasion became a regular course of study at school. Any attempt for protection—even the absurd notion to cover oneself with vines to hide from bombers—was taken seriously.

Flyers were distributed by the Neighborhood Associations instructing residents on the constant changes in the system of air raid sirens. One long hoot lasting a minute meant that enemy bombers have invaded Japanese airspace. This would be followed by ten short hoots indicating the air raid was about to begin. After the raid, one long siren signaled the all clear.

Newspapers maintained a steady beat of patriotism printing the Imperial Prescript every day and were filled with headlines of false bravado like, *Japan is girding itself for a knockout blow!* The nation was instructed that only *sacrifice* would stave off the inevitable assault of the *white-skinned devils.*

Hiryo Fujiyama, who trained pilots at the Kanoya Naval Base, was to experience this sacrifice in its most abhorrent form—and first-hand. "I can't believe the General Staff would agree to the formation and use of the Special Attack Force," Hiryo uttered to Admiral Ugaki in the flight ready hut.

"First," Ugaki replied, "let me give you my condolences on the courageous death of your father. He was a great, great man and a brave warrior as well."

"Hai," Hiryo replied, bowing his head.

"As for the General Staff," Ugaki began, "they originally rejected the idea of the Special Attack Force as a waste of pilots and a danger to moral. But, in fact, it was actually a tactic demanded by junior officers who saw that they could not match the rising power of American air and naval power. And I agreed with them."

Ugaki paused a moment and looked above his head as a hard rain began to ping loudly upon the tin roof of the flight ready hut. "The Divine Wind—the kamikaze—is our only weapon against the might of the American navy, and specifically, their aircraft carriers."

Hiryo nodded. "Hai. Without their carriers, the Americans could not island hop toward Japan."

The two men fell silent in mutual agreement before Ugaki spoke once again. "Iwo Jima is about to fall to the Americans. Then Okinawa will be next." He placed his hand upon Hiryo's shoulder. "The young men you are training are volunteers. They will be our most effective weapon against the American fleet when they arrive off of Okinawa. Our young pilots must do this willingly... for their county and their family." He lowered his voice. "Human life is precious, but we must not avoid sacrifices to win the war."

"And dying for the Emperor, too?" Hiryo added, his voice dripping with sarcasm, not caring what Ugaki might think.

But the Admiral did not react. Perhaps he too could see the madness of pursuing a war that would eventually destroy his country, or perhaps his attitude was only fatalistic.

"But you have my word that I will train my pilots to the best of their ability, sir," Hiryo added.

Ugaki just grunted, picked up his hat and prepared to leave the flight control hut.

Hiryo stood at attention and gave the Admiral a salute.

"I know you will do your duty, Captain," he noted with little ceremony. "We *all* will when the time comes. Anything less would be unacceptable."

Horror in Manchukuo

My diplomatic flight from Nanking landed in Changchun, the capital of Manchukuo, which was located a hundred or so kilometers from the Kwantung peninsula. As a courtesy, the German Consulate in Changchun provided me with a car, and during the ride to the village, I was filled with hopes of finding out what Father Marquette knew of Unit 731.

A German Consular aide met me at the airport and showed me to my vehicle. "It will take you the better part of a day to reach the village," the aide stated. "Why the diplomatic visit?"

I responded with some vague half-truths and misdirection that seemed to satisfy the aide and was soon alone on my way.

Dark columns of angry clouds laced with streaks of lightning chased me as I drove over the uneven dirt roads towards my destination. I arrived at the settlement just before dusk, barely beating the storm that had been following me. I began my quest in the village on foot as the first heavy drops of rain fell upon the German Army wool coat I borrowed at the consulate. My memory from my last visit stood murky in my mind, nothing looked familiar as I tried to remember where the priest's hut was located.

It was getting dark and I feared I might not find my destination in the dimming light, so I knocked on the next hut I came across in the hopes of someone knowing where the French priest lived. An ancient looking Manchu man cracked open the door and stared at my German coat with distrustful eyes. I asked him through the tiny gap in the door if he knew where Father Marquette lived. The old man scratched at his patchy beard as if considering if I was worth his time. Finally, he nodded, then without speaking, he led me to an area behind the village.

We stopped on a rough patch of land pitted with small mounds of dirt, and the old man pointed north. I gazed in that direction, and after seeing nothing, I turned back to the old man, but he was gone.

"He is dead," a voice came from out of the shadows behind me.

I turned as a figure emerged from the falling mist. It was Huan Quang, the peasant who was with Marquette the day I had met him.

"The Kempeitai came in the night," Quang said bitterly. "Pulled him from his home and shot him in the head."

My stomach sunk at the news—another lead snatched from me just as I was about to close in on my elusive objective. "Why? Why did they kill him?"

"I would imagine for the very same reason you are here. The Epidemic Prevention and Water Purification Department."

My mind was sent reeling. "Unit 731?"

Quang merely nodded.

"Father Marquette's note to me said he knew where this Department...where Unit 731 was located." I swallowed hard. "Would you happen to know?"

"Yes."

And before I could respond, Quang gestured for me to follow him. "Come. I'll show you."

✳ ✳ ✳

The rain had finally stopped, and we drove through most of the night before arriving at the foot of a small ridge. I followed Quang's lead to the crest and stared into the darkness, lit only by the full moon breaking through the dissipating clouds of the former storm. I could only make out indistinguishable shapes scattered over the ground. "What are those?"

129

Quang said nothing and continued to lead me forward until I tripped against an object at me feet. I looked down and recoiled in horror at a grotesque corpse, hollow eyes wide open, staring up at me.

"Manchu," Quang said and pointed out hundreds of other corpses that were strewn over the ground that led to a small village in the distance. "All Manchus. A village full of them. Men. Women. Children. All murdered by the Japanese," he sneered. "Murdered by the Kempeitai. Murdered by Unit 731."

"I-I don't... I don't understand," I whispered. "How—?"

"Plague," he said in disgust. "Unit 731 is a biological weapons factory, Mr. Reporter. That village there was a test site for their latest bio-weapon."

I could hardly believe my ears. The thought of the stolen gold was forgotten in the face of this horrendous, inhuman act.

Quang grabbed my arm. "You are a reporter. *You* have to tell the world of this. Of what the Japanese are doing here."

I could only nod my head. This was monstrous—far beyond any war crimes I had witnessed the Japanese military commit before. I clenched my teeth. "Yes. I'll do my best. I—"

Quang's hand quickly shot up and clapped it over my mouth. "They're coming," he whispered and pointed to our left.

I looked over to see soldiers covered from head to toe in silver suites walking among the Manchu bodies, occasionally bending down and cutting samples from the dead.

"We have to go. *Now!*" Quang whispered.

As we turned, I tripped over a corpse and toppled to the ground. Quang yanked me back to my feet and dragged me from the scene.

I glanced back over my shoulder and watched as two silvery soldiers pointed in our direction and shouldered their rifles.

We ran blindly in the dark towards the car, over corpses and through the trees. I could smell Quang's fear. When we finally reached my car, I started the engine, praying we would not run into any other soldiers, and sped away into the night.

✳ ✳ ✳

I left Quang at the priest's village and drove back to my hotel. I was scheduled to be on the return flight to Nanking that evening. Still numbed at what I had witnessed, I gathered my thoughts and sat down to type up what I had seen of the monstrosity of Unit 731.

An hour later, I finished my report and addressed an envelope to the Assistant to the Lord Keeper of the Privy Seal of Japan—His Excellency Kenta Hiyakawa. I then placed my report into a second envelope, sealed it and wrote: 'To Tomoko Sakura. Managing Editor. *Tokyo Nichinichi Shimbu*—Private'. I placed that envelope into the one addressed to Hiyakawa.

I prepared for bed, fully expecting my exhaustion to coax me into a deep slumber, but that night, I found sleep to be utterly evasive.

A Devastating Loss

It was a mild and windy night in Tokyo the first week of March 1945, and Connor and Aiko made good use of the conditions cuddling together in her room at the geisha house. All the worries that troubled Connor's mind since arriving in Japan were soon soothed by Aiko's love and attention.

It was like his life had begun anew.

Lying next to Connor on her bed, Aiko rested her head on his shoulder when he once again urged her to leave Tokyo with him.

"That's impossible, Connor-san," she replied.

As Connor was about to argue the point, he heard heavy thumping footsteps on the stairs below.

Aiko shot from the bed just as the bedroom door crashed open and Matsumura's sumo guard filled the entire doorframe.

The sumo stumped across the room, reached down toward Connor, and yanked him out of the bed by his throat. As he dangled the boy in the air, Aiko screamed and pleaded to the giant for mercy.

"Too late for that," Matsumura offered as he entered the room.

Seeing her Master, Aiko threw herself at his feet. "Please, Matsumura. Don't hurt him!"

He glared down at Aiko and seemed disgusted by her pathetic display. "He will not hurt him." He nodded to the sumo. "He will *kill* him."

Aiko's screams of protest were ignored as the sumo squeezed

his hands around Connor's throat, slowly crushing the life from his body.

Matsumura watched on as Connor's legs kicked and thrashed, and his hand scratched at the big man's face in the futile attempt to escape his clutches.

Aiko stood up and threw herself at the sumo, but he merely swatted her aside like an irritant insect and continued his death grip upon the young American.

As Connor's body started to grow limp, the huge bulk of the man unconsciously loosened his grip, cocked his head, and looked up at the ceiling listening to an ever growing drone of heavy airplane engines just over his head. A beat later, the window in Aiko's room suddenly shattered, sending shards of glass, chunks of wood and streaks of fire hurtling inside.

The shock forced the sumo to drop Connor to the floor, and before he could gather his wits, the entire ceiling of the room erupted in flames.

Connor stood up, grabbed Aiko by the arm, and pulled her towards the door. He shoved passed Matsumura, who stood frozen in shock, and dragged Aiko down blazing stairs.

They could hear the stomping of heavy footsteps behind them as the sumo gave chase through the inferno. Connor braved a glance over his shoulder, only to see the stairs give way, collapsing in a flaming heap under the sumo who was then immediately engulfed in the fire. He could only guess at Matsumura's fate.

Connor and Aiko stumbled out of the geisha house, eyes and lungs burning from choking smoke.

Through bleary tears, Connor peered up to the sky and saw beams of anti-aircraft lights probing the night, illuminating billowing puffs of grey smoke from exploding *ack-ack* fire. The sky appeared sown with fire, and the bright light parted the night revealing B-29s in the sky. Their long, glinting wings, sharp as blades, reflected the fire from the furnace below.

Connor shouted, "They're fire-bombing Tokyo..."

The B-29 bombers, their silver forms oddly beautifully illuminated against the searchlights, dropped bombs from their underbelly. The weapons, looking like fireflies in the sky, soon erupted into hairs of flame as they plummeted towards the ground.

A violent wind created by the firestorm began to sweep up the burning debris, filling the air with live sparks, then with burning bits of wood and paper until it manifested into a raining torrent of fire.

Connor and Aiko rushed through the panic of the city as a horrid breath of fire swirled and sucked whole blocks of houses into a maelstrom of misery and suffering. Roofs of homes collapsed under massive waves of flames, lighted from the inside like paper lanterns. Fiery debris hurtled through the air from explosions, severing people in half and setting fire to whatever else it touched.

A woman stumbled from the burning wreckage of her home, screaming and pleading for help. "My baby is inside! My baby..."

They watched as the woman turned and ran back inside the inferno. Then Aiko broke from Connor's side and raced toward the crumbling structure.

"Aiko!" Connor screamed. "Aiko! Come back!" But he was cut off as the home completely collapsed, sending towering spikes of flames into the air.

Aiko dropped to the ground, screaming and crying from the horror all around her.

"There's nothing we can do," Connor urged as he pulled her back to her feet. "Come. We have to make it to the river."

Aiko reluctantly allowed Connor to guide her away from the devastation. They continued down the street, pushing and shoving their way through the throng of terrified people as policemen and firemen tried in vain to control the fleeing crowds that stampeded past them.

Connor led Aiko down a side street. Flaming paper houses literally exploded into flames on both sides of them. He attempted to shield Aiko's eyes from the horrible scene before them—men, women and children thrashing on the ground in the futile attempt to extinguish the flames that blackened their flesh.

It was all Connor and Aiko could do to keep from vomiting.

They pressed on, passing stalled fire engines, out of fuel and unable to move as the wind blew through the city, whipping up the flames higher and higher and burning more and more people alive.

It was a living hell.

Nineteen square miles of Tokyo stood ablaze as they staggered through the carnage and finally made it to the Meguro River that ran to the bay. The ever-mounting waves of people pressed into the narrow strips of land under a bridge, pushed irresistibly toward the river as entire walls of screaming humanity toppled over and disappeared in the deep water.

At the bridge, human clusters of terrified citizens clung to the steel railings until the heat became too unbearable to hold, and bodies dropped like falling, rotted fruit. Connor felt heat consume his feet and legs, and as he stared down, he noticed their shoes and clothing were smoldering.

"I can't... I can't... breathe..." Aiko gasped. "It's too hot..."

Connor stared down at the boiling water. Countless bodies floated in the rivet—all black as charcoal.

"Aiko! No!" he screamed, as she climbed onto the bridge and readied herself to jump into the river.

But his pleas were too late. Aiko threw herself toward the steaming river before Connor could reach out and restrain her.

She screamed as she plunged into the turbulent waters, but the boiling water quickly filled her lungs and silenced her cries.

Connor stared into the dark abyss below as his screams of desperation and horror obscured the explosion of firebombs that detonated all around him.

A Shocking Announcement

At dawn on April 7th, the battleship *Yamato* churned south from Kyushu towards Okinawa. On board Vice-Admiral Seiichi Ito stood in command of Operation Ten-Go in a desperate defense of the island. The *Yamato* and heavy cruiser *Yahagi* were encircled by a ring of eight destroyers as the task force steamed south.

A yeoman delivered a message for Kosaku Aruga, Captain of the *Yamato*, and gave it to Daiki at the helm.

"Read it," Aruga instructed.

Daiki clutched the report and read aloud. "The damage control drills have been completed."

"Hai. That is good."

But Aruga noticed the concerned etched upon Daiki's face. "What is it, helmsman?"

"Sir. All these intense damage-control drills," Daiki replied in a puzzled voice. "It is much more than standard practice."

"And?"

"The rumors, sir. The rumors are that this ship is being prepared to be sacrificed."

Aruga stood silent for a few moments, then walked directly to the intercom on the bridge. "It's time the crew knows our mission."

Daiki watched silently as Aruga clutched the mic and composed himself before speaking.

"Attention to all crew of the *Yamato*. Your attention, please," the Captain began. He took a deep breath. "Our orders are to fight our way to Okinawa through the American fleet, then beach our ship and use it as shore batteries against the American invasion until our guns are destroyed. After that, we will abandon the *Yamato* and fight the Americans on land. That is all." Aruga turned and saw the shock in Daiki's eyes.

"Helmsman, this proud ship is now part of the Special Attack Force. It will be followed by special attacks from the air against the American fleet. A Divine Wind."

He placed his hand on Daiki's shoulder. "This ship will do its duty, and so will its crew." He dropped his hand and stared out over the open sea. "Now. Take us to Okinawa."

Death of an Icon

"Enemy aircraft!" shouted the lookout on the bridge.

Daiki snapped to where the sailor indicated. Off to the right of the high noon sun he spotted a flight of American dive-bombers and torpedo planes and additional planes he hadn't seen before. "What are those?" he asked to no one in particular on the bridge.

"Corsairs," Aruga replied. "The *new* American fighters."

A moment later, Admiral Ito entered the bridge. "Status, Captain?" he inquired coolly.

Aruga pointed to the American planes hovering above their ships. "The Americans realize we have no air cover. They're circling our ship formation and setting up their attacks just out of range of our anti-aircraft guns."

Ito stared at the American air fleet above them and whispered to Aruga. "What are they waiting for?"

As if in direct response to the Admiral's question, the American planes moved in unison, descending upon the *Yamato* and unleashing their attack.

"Increase speed to twenty-four knots," Aruba barked. "Begin evasive maneuvers. Engage anti-aircraft guns. Main batteries open fire!"

As Daiki steered the ship as Aruga ordered, he noticed the torpedo planes were attacking only on the port side of the ship and wondered why.

His question was answered a split second later.

"They're attempting to capsize the ship," Ito said. "Direct all anti-aircraft fire towards the enemy torpedo planes."

The evasive maneuvers ordered by Aruga proved successful. Only two armor piercing bombs and one torpedo made direct hits on the *Yamato*, but one of the bombs started a heavy fire aft of the superstructure that quickly burned out of control.

"Change course 180 degrees," Aruga barked at Daiki.

But the *Yamato's* time appeared to be drawing to a close.

The American dive-bombers and torpedo planes swarmed over and around the ship like angry, deadly hornets, causing extensive damage throughout the vessel.

After several explosions rocked the groaning ship, Ito snapped toward Aruga. "Damage report, Captain."

"Extensive damage to the top side of the ship caused by multiple torpedo hits and bombs. Power knocked out to the gun directors. The anti-aircraft guns can now only be used manually, sir, greatly reducing their effectiveness." He sighed wearily, fighting to retain his composure. "The torpedo hits are listing the ship severely to port. Capsizing is an imminent danger."

"Can we counter flood to compensate for the list?" Ito asked.

Aruga shook his head. "No, sir. The water damage control system was damaged by a bomb hit. We cannot compensate." He lowered his voice. "It's over."

Ito nodded. "We have no other choices. Flood the starboard engine and boiler rooms."

Aruga knew the implications of the order. Several hundred crewmen would be instantly drowned by the action. Almost immediately after giving the order, the *Yamato* appeared to bog down and grow sluggish.

"Sir. We're slowing!" Daiki shouted. "I can't keep her up to speed."

"It's the water we're taking on," the Captain replied. "Do your best, helmsman. Do your best."

The *Yamato* eventually slowed to a crawl—it's speed gradually reducing to less than ten knots. It now stood as an easy target for the swarms of American planes ready to pounce and obliterate the stricken ship. Twenty American torpedo planes made runs again to port as three torpedoes ripped into the steel of her port side.

Daiki fought the steering, but it was a futile effort. "Sir," he cried. "The rudder is jammed to port."

"We're circling," Ito said. "Cancel the mission. Abandon ship. Inform the other ships to pick up survivors."

"Sir," Aruga replied and shook his head. "Our radio system is out."

"Then use signal flags," Ito growled as the huge bulk of the flaming ship stopped dead in the water and began to list severely to port.

"You heard the order," Aruga barked at Daiki. "Abandon ship." He then looked over at Admiral Ito, a silent understanding passing between the two men, and nodded. "Go. The Admiral and I are staying."

"Sir. I..."

"Go!" Aruga snapped a final time.

Daiki left the tilting bridge and pushed his way through the melee of crewmen attempting to climb aboard lifeboats, but the mass hysteria made it impossible. Daiki stood on the railing above a half full lifeboat and was about to jump when a series of large explosion rocked the entire ship and tossed him overboard.

Daiki crashed into the water and sank several feet until he was finally able to claw his way back to the surface. Through eyes stinging from the salt water, he found he was being carried away from the capsizing *Yamato* by massive, undulating waves.

As he searched for a rescue boat, the *Yamato* suddenly blew up with an explosion so immense and powerful, that it sucked him under water for several agonizing moments. When he burst to the surface, all he could see was a large mushroom-shaped cloud climbing 20,000 feet in the air.

Daiki thrashed in the water until he found what was left of a shattered lifeboat, grabbed a piece of jagged wood, and hung on for dear life.

He bobbed aimlessly in the water, spitting salt water from

burning lungs, recoiling in horror as chunks of seared body parts floated passed—and prayed.

Hopelessness and Despair

Over a period of several weeks, blinded by hopelessness and despair, Connor trudged through the charred remains of the city to places he and Aiko had visited when their hearts and minds were filled only with love and joy. But every spot—restaurants, parks, specific street corners—had been left burnt and scarred by the atrocity of war.

Connor's emotional trek led him to the foot of Mt. Fuji where Aiko shared the traditional tea ceremony with him.

He spent some time at the picnic site, then, after a while, his seemingly pointless journey led him to a sign that held some fascination for him that day. The sign was etched into a piece of wood and attached to the side of a century-old tree. The simple words seemed to know the steadfast feeling arising from the center of his entire being.

Your life is a precious gift from your parents. Don't throw it away.

Yes, he thought. But how could he live without the gift of Aiko? Aiko, who saved him from his lonely alienation.

Walking in a despondent daze, he arrived at the Aokigaharathe. Sea of Trees. The Demon Forest. The Suicide Forest.

Without thinking and without hesitation, he entered the wood so thick and dense, even in the high noon sun it was shrouded almost in absolute darkness. Rocky and cold, it was devoid of any sound except that of his steps cracking the volcanic floor beneath his feet.

Aiko had told him of the cursed forest, haunted by the *yurei*—the angry, lonely spirits of those who had taken their lives upon the soil.

Yes. It is the perfect place to die.

Though weakened by hunger, as he hadn't eaten anything of substance in days, Connor made his way through the thick patches of trees with its twisting network of woody vines and the dangerous terrain of the forest floor. With his mind slipping to another place, another time, Connor snagged his foot over a gnarled root, toppled forward, and rolled down a small, stony hill.

He finally landed with a grunt upon a soft, dense object, and stared into face of a rotting corpse. He screamed, scrambled to his feet, and ran face-first into a skeleton dangling from a tree. He slowly backed away from the carcass, then bumped into another corpse, then another hanging from the trees. He stopped and stared at a half-dozen badly decomposed bodies hanging in front of him—all ripped and torn apart by the beaks of carrion birds.

Dehydrated and malnourished from his lack of food and drink that he had no appetite for, he stumbled through the human foliage and took refuge in a large ice cave—one of many created by lava flows from Mt. Fuji. Columns of ice three feet in diameter rose from the floor of the cave and connected to the icy ceiling.

He halted in his tracks as a large shape sped past his line of sight.

An animal? A large predator?

Then, through the dim, muted light, white, twisting forms glided from darkness before him. Were they real, or were exhaustion, despair, and the lack of light playing tricks on him?

He shook the images from his head, determined to accomplish one final deed—to end his life of misery. The misery of his nanny's and Fujiyama's death. The misery of his alienation. The misery of his lost love. The very misery of living.

He inched his way deeper into the cave until reaching a ledge with nothing but darkness below. He teetered at the precipice, willing himself to make one final step, to end his absolute despair. As his foot stepped forward over the abyss, a figure appeared, looking like a stonewall, but with a pair of arms and legs.

Nurikabe, he whispered under his breath.

Was his mind once again playing tricks on him? It was the very same mythical creature Miyoko told him about. The creature that blocked his way.

"Connor?" the apparition whispered.

Connor began to back way from the illusion.

"Connor?" the apparition whispered yet again.

Connor rubbed his eyes as the specter came into focus. To his surprise it was Jiro.

"Jiro? What are you doing here?" Connor gasped.

"I followed you here. I needed to talk to you. Come. Let's leave this horrid place."

Connor felt his arm being pulled away from the edge of the icy ridge, back through the cave, and finally out into the light.

As Connor's eyes adjusted, Jiro reached out and placed his hand on the American's shoulder. "I heard about Aiko. I'm sorry. So, so sorry."

"What do you want?" Connor finally managed to ask.

"I want you to join us. Join us to kill the Americans. Join us to avenge your Aiko."

Connor just shook his head. He was confused. His thoughts were as clouded as they ever were about his past and present.

"Your family is in danger from the Americans. They will kill them. You owe it to your family to defend them," Jiro urged. "It's up to you to keep Miyoko, Suki, and Kenji from harm."

Those were almost the same exact words Fujiyama used when he made Connor promise to protect his family.

"Will you join us, Connor-san?"

Ketsugo

Hiyakawa nodded to the receptionist for the Lord Keeper of the Privy Seal and entered into Kido's office.

Kido sat behind his desk and motioned to the door. "Close the door, Kenta," Kido softly requested. "Have a seat."

Hiyakawa positioned himself in a chair opposite Kido's large teak desk and waited patiently for Lord Keeper to begin.

"The War Cabinet has met," Kido finally stated. "Prime Minister Suzuki announced that Japan will fight to the very end rather than accept unconditional surrender."

"I don't understand. The Emperor demanded a *tennozan*—a great victory. The military did *not* deliver it. Okinawa has fallen to the Americans."

Kido merely nodded.

"And what was the Emperor's response to these facts?"

"He is following through with *Ketsugo*. To fight with spiritual strength. He and the military are determined to resist. We will bleed the Americans to force a negotiated peace and there will be no surrender."

Hiyakawa sat speechless, his mind racing with frustration and barely contained anger.

Kido glanced out his office window before continuing. "Every Japanese man, woman, and child is ordered to die in defense of the homeland. There are to be no exceptions."

"Madness," Hiyakawa finally snapped. "Unbelievable. Our fleet is largely destroyed. The seas surrounding Japan are ruled by American warships. Their bombers and fighter planes fly unopposed and attack our factories and railroads at will. Rationing of food is at starvation levels. How can one fight with spiritual strength without anything to eat!"

Hiyakawa could no longer remain seated. He burst from his chair and paced the office floor. "I've witnessed our citizens overjoyed at the sight of a noodle or a bean at the bottom of a soup bowl. If the defeat of Japan is the inevitable outcome, why not surrender and attempt to resume some semblance of life?"

"Because the military simply doesn't see it that way." Kido stood up and walked over to Hiyakawa. "The military still has powerful forces in the field, especially in Manchuria and China. They can be brought back to defend the homeland."

Hiyakawa sighed bitterly and shook his head. "False hopes. Nothing more."

Kido sat against the edge of his desk and placed his hands in his lap. "We must attempt to be strong, my friend, and support the decision of the Cabinet."

Hiyakawa placed his hand on the door handle, then stopped and looked back at Kido. "This was the outcome we all feared would happen in 1941. One we were unable to prevent. And now it is upon us."

Got Them

"And this was supposed to be delivered to Marque Hiyakawa?" Sato asked one of the staff of Kido's office.

The little staff member nodded, and held a small pouch in his hands. "Hai. A diplomatic pouch from the German Embassy in Nanking."

Sato removed the pouch from the staff member's hands and settled into his seat behind his desk. "I'll take care of it from here."

"But, sir. I have to deliver it to..."

Sato glared at the little bureaucrat, and the man simply bowed and retreated quickly from the office.

Sato opened the pouch and withdrew an envelope marked *To Tomoko Sakura. Managing Editor. Tokyo Nichinichi Shimbun—Private.*

He tore open the envelope, unfolded the slip of paper, and read the report on Unit 731. A slow, deliberate smile creased his lips.

"Got them," he whispered.

The Final Straw

"*And our gallant Imperial Air Force successfully destroyed one hundred bombers last night over Kyoto. In other war news...*"

Miyoko finally had heard enough of the propaganda and snapped off the radio. "Kenji," she called down the hall. "Get ready for school."

Kenji entered the kitchen and handed his mother a stack of unopened mail. "What was that thundering noise we heard in the distance last night?"

"One of the neighbors said it was Allied naval bombardment south of Shingu," she replied as she sorted through the mail. "Sumisu-san down the street claimed the American guns destroyed a factory and that many civilians were also killed by the shells."

"Will the Americans shell us, too?"

Miyoko shook her head and opened an official looking envelope. "I don't know. So far Hiroshima has been spared from any air raids."

"I hope it stays that way," Kenji remarked. "Do you think it will?"

But Miyoko was not listening. Her faced drained of all color and her eyes began to well up.

"What's wrong, Mama-san?"

She did not respond. Instead, she merely held up a red card in her trembling hand.

Kenji didn't need to read the card to know exactly what is was—a *draft notice.*

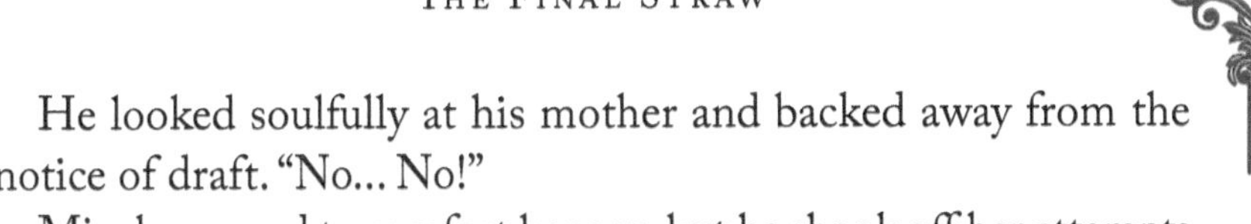

He looked soulfully at his mother and backed away from the notice of draft. "No... No!"

Miyoko moved to comfort her son, but he shook off her attempts. "I won't go!" he screamed. "I won't go!" And he ran crying from the house, bowling past Connor, who had just entered.

"What's wrong with Kenji?" Connor asked, watching the young boy bolt out of the house.

"Oh, Connor-san. You are alive!" And she ran to her American son, clutching him in a tight embrace. "We heard of Aiko's death and feared you were killed in the fire bombing yourself."

Connor broke down in tears and pressed his face against her cheek. "Mama-san... she's gone. *Gone*. It was horrible." And the horrid memories of that terrible night came rushing back to him.

They stood there for several moments, hugging and comforting each other.

"Tell me, what's the matter with Kenji," he finally said.

She wiped the tears from her face with a small handkerchief. "He received his draft notice today."

He knew exactly what Miyoko was thinking.

Blackpatch.

"Don't worry, Mama-san. I'll find him."

Connor gave his adopted mother one last hug and left quickly to find his Japanese brother.

He went straight to the main Hiroshima train station and pushed himself through the morning throng of commuters.

A train approached from the east, and Connor shoved his way to the edge of the platform. He looked left, then right, but didn't see Kenji lined up in the queue. He searched across the tracks to the opposite platform, but Kenji wasn't there either.

Feeling an overwhelming sense of relief, Connor walked towards the exit when he spotted Kenji walking on the tracks—a train was fast approaching right in his direction.

Connor pushed his way through the crowd, bowling over several men and women, and leapt down onto the tracks. "Kenji! Stop!"

Kenji turned at the sound of his name and just stared at Connor. Then, after a moment, he turned and walked towards the looming train.

Connor caught up with him and grabbed him by the arm. "I won't let you do this."

"Let me go, Connor! I'm not going. *I'm not going*," he cried.

"Then I'll stay here with you," Connor replied.

"But you'll die!"

"So be it."

Kenji burst into tears and threw his arms around Connor as the train, blaring a warning, bored down closer to the two boys.

"If you die, I die with you," Connor whispered.

Kenji shook his head and pulled them both from the tracks as the train came screaming past them.

They stood upon the dirt, clutching at one another, both submitting to angry, relieved tears. Connor finally squeezed his brother's shoulder. "Let's go home."

Kenji nodded, and as they walked, they were stopped by the shrill sound of a silver fighter plane soaring above them.

"What kind of plane is that?" Connor asked.

Kenji wiped the tears from his eyes and focused upon the plane. "That's one of the American's new fighters. A P-51 Mustang!" he squealed.

As the two boys watched, the P-51 abruptly dropped in altitude, and in a blur of motion, it began strafing the train station.

"Get down!" Connor screamed and pulled Kenji to the ground.

The two boys watched from their prone position as the fighter completed its attack, gained altitude and returned for another run.

"We have to get out of here!" Connor cried.

The two boys stood and ran from the station as the mayhem of explosions and screams filled the air around them.

The P-51 soared over the station again, strafing it as it passed, then went down the tracks after the passing train towards Kenji and Connor, spitting up bits of rock and dirt around the two boys.

Connor once again hit the dirt and watched as the fighter disappeared over the horizon. When he looked at Kenji, he noticed the pool of crimson liquid flowing from his brother's head.

Connor crawled across the rocks and knelt by his side.

"Kenji? *Kenji?!*"

He pulled his brother into his lap, gently checked his neck for a pulse, then gazed into Kenji's lifeless eyes. "Please wake up, Kenji... please..." Then Connor's tears began to flow and he cried harder than he had ever cried before.

Shock and Dismay

I arrived in Tokyo in mid-July of 1945 and was shocked at what I witnessed. I'd watched the news reports of the fire bombing in March and the continued bombing of Tokyo and other cities over the last few months, but it did little to prepare me for what stood all around me.

As I drove through the city by cab—miraculously some of them were still operating—a large portion of Tokyo was demolished, and the stench of smoke and burnt wood filled the city air.

That terrible night of horror and devastation in March burned through almost twenty square miles of the proud city. Due to its densely populated wooden homes and buildings, the raging infernos created the most destructive weapon of all—the firestorm.

I read stories of men, women, and children huddled in underground shelters, roasted alive by the firestorm that raged above them—fires that could be seen 150 miles away. Entire families perished in holes they had dug under their wooden houses in hopes of refuge, but instead, their makeshift shelters collapsed and incinerated them in their holes.

Estimates of the number killed ranged from 80,000 to 200,000.

Angry and bitter at both the militarists that pulled us into this war and the Americans whose fighters and bombers raked the skies at will, I arrived at the building where my newspaper resided. The building stood severely damaged, but it was being repaired by service people as if such repairs were an everyday occurrence.

The moment I entered the newspaper offices, my stomach sank.

Standing in the pressroom next to Sakura, who appeared frail and unsteady, was Sato with two Tokkō police. I immediately noticed that Sato clutched my report on Unit 731 in his hand.

"Ah. Just the man we wanted to see. We've been waiting for you, Mr. Koga," Sato smirked. The Kempeitai Colonel used the American salutation. It was a foreboding sign.

He slowly waved my report in the air. "This is traitorous, Mr. Koga. You betray your country." He carefully folded my report and let it drop to the floor. "And this is how we deal with traitors." He drew his sidearm, leveled the barrel at me pointblank, then quickly turned and fired a round at Sakura.

Sakura staggered backwards, grasped the growing red stain on his chest, looked at me for one brief instant, then fell dead on the spot.

My legs buckled beneath me, and I thumped to the floor.

"As for you, Mr. Koga," Sato whispered, "I have something more traditional in mind for traitors." He nodded to one of the Tokkō police. "Take him away.

Keeping the Promise

Miyoko listened to the latest news in the kitchen accompanied by the ever-present martial music. Though the news was filed with threats on how Japan would defeat the Allies approaching their shore, Miyoko knew that the enemy was turning Japan's cities into scorched ruin. And she knew that soon, with the inevitable invasion, the direst of consequences would fall upon her country.

She heard footsteps traipse down the hallway, and turned to see Connor standing alongside Jiro. Her mouth opened to greet her American son, but Connor's cold expression sent a shiver of dread through her body.

"Mama-san," Connor said, "I am leaving. I must keep my promise to Fujiyama. My promise to protect my family."

"I don't understand," Miyoko replied. "You can't join the military. They won't allow it."

Jiro responded for Connor instead. "There are better ways to defend our families and our country. Better ways than what the military can do now."

Connor reached out for his mother's soft hand and squeezed it tenderly. "Too many have died. And for nothing. My nanny. Yoshi. Fujiyama. And now Kenji. The Americans will not stop until they kill us all." He gazed into his adopted mother's sad eyes. "They need pilots. Pilots with flying experience. That's the only way I can keep you and Suki safe."

Miyoko began to weep. Her entire body shook, and she shook her head back and forth. "No, Connor-san. That is not the only way..."

Connor bowed his head and shook his head as well. "This is no time to think selfishly of one's life."

The Firing Squad

Later that evening, I found myself contained in what was left of one of the local police station's cells. Though it was a local police precinct, out of the way from the city center, it was a bustle of activity, and the activity did not bode well.

"Koga!" a voice barked as a man approached my cell. "It seems your curiosity has gotten the best of you this time," Major Takahashi scoffed. He was flanked by two armed Japanese soldiers at his side, and they were decked out in full battle gear.

I recognized them immediately—*Kwantung troops.*

I stared at the soldiers for a moment before turning my attention back on Takahashi. "What are Kwantung soldiers doing in Tokyo?"

"To deal with traitors like you." He moved closer to my cell and pressed his face against the steel bars.

"*Americans* like you." He peered around my cell before locking his eyes on mine. "You leave for our command center in Hiroshima soon. We mustn't keep the firing squad waiting."

Meaning

"You made the right decision," Jiro confided to Connor. The two boys sat in the headquarters office of Admiral Ugaki, and had been waiting for quite some time. "There is much honor in what we are doing."

Connor nodded to project a determined response, but he wasn't less interested in pursuing honor than pursuing *justice*.

As Jiro rambled on about the glory to come, Connor heard his name called. A young naval ensign approached and asked Connor to follow him.

A few moments later, Connor stood in front of an Admiral of the Imperial Navy, impeccably dressed in a crisp white uniform adorned with colorful battle ribbons and other honors earned during his career. Connor knew of Ugaki. Fujiyama had shared the Admiral's near death experience flying on the fateful day that killed Yamamoto.

"Have a seat," Ugaki instructed.

Connor complied, sitting in a hard metal chair opposite the Admiral's grey metal desk.

Ugaki lit a cigarette and spent a few minutes leafing through a file in front of him, his dour expression barely changing. Finally, he closed the file and leveled his gaze upon Connor. "I don't frankly understand," he began. "You are an American. Why would you want to kill your own people?"

"I am half Japanese," Connor corrected and pointed to the

application papers on the Admiral's desk. "It's all in there. Everything about me."

Ugaki nodded. "I worked with your father. Fujiyama was a good man and a great warrior." His eyes bore deep into Connor's as if searching for justification and hidden truth. "But that doesn't explain why you want to kill Americans, and ultimately yourself."

Connor nodded solemnly, fully expecting this exact question. "The Americans are killing my Japanese family. They're killing the people I love most. Isn't that enough?"

Ugaki grunted, leaned back in his chair and lit another cigarette before realizing one was already smoldering in the ashtray on his desk. "Everyone of our pilots have their own reasons for becoming a Divine Wind. Some pledge to die for the Emperor, some for our country, but many are like you. They accept the honor to defend their families." He turned his chair around and stared out his window, exhaling a plume of fine smoke. "We are losing this war. We will soon be at the mercy of the Americans if we don't stop them."

Ugaki turned back towards Connor and stabbed his cigarette into an ashtray overflowing with other butts. "I believe the Kamikaze can do that. During the sea battle at Okinawa alone, Japanese Kamikaze aircraft sank thirty-two Allied ships and damaged more than four hundred others. If we can wear the Americans down, make them tired of this war and of their own casualties, then perhaps we can sue for peace, retain the Emperor, avoid an occupation, and place disarmament and any trials of war criminals in the hands of our military."

As he summarized his thoughts, he slammed his hand on top of the desk. "If we can do that, we may keep our country!"

"Sir," Connor pleaded. "I have little meaning in my life. Everything I believed in, everything I have ever loved, has been taken from me. I want my life to mean something. Protecting what's left of my family *is* that meaning. I want to join the Divine Wind."

Ugaki sat silent for a few moments before replying. He finally nodded, his jaw set hard. "Fine. Report to our airbase at Kisarazu. I'll have the ensign outside cut your orders."

Connor snapped to his feet and gave Ugaki a robust salute. "Thank you, sir."

Operation Ketsu-Go

"**N**o!" Prince Chichibu barked. "This is not acceptable," the Prince pounded on Marquis Kōichi Kido's draft document.

"But the Emperor wants us to consider the proposed settlement," Kido countered. "He has met with the ministers and said he desired concrete plans to end the war, unhampered by existing policy, and to speedily study them and efforts be made to implement them."

"No! We must continue the war!" Prince Chichibu spat furiously.

Kido stood his ground and wouldn't back down before the Prince's flaring rage. "We can send emissaries to Russia and ask them to interceded for us. We can ask them to help us negotiate an equitable surrender."

"Our only choice is to fight on and deal the American invasion a mortal blow," the Prince uttered. He shuffled through a stack of some materials in front of him and withdrew a thick folder labeled *Top Secret*. "Operation Ketsu-Go," he growled, waving the Top Secret folder in front of Kido. "We are *not* defeated."

Hiyakawa, who had sat silent up until this point, merely shook his head at the rhetoric he heard. The extent to which the government maintained blanket denial of the reality of the war was unbelievable.

The Prince continued his rant. "We can make the Americans pay for the invasion of our islands. We have built secret suicide takeoff strips and underground hangers, camouflaged airfields and seaplane bases to launch Kamikaze attacks on the American fleet. We still have over twelve thousand army and navy aircraft. Preparations are underway in every corner of Japan—hidden in underground mines, railway tunnels, under viaducts, and in basements of department stores. Work is being done every single day to construct new planes."

He slammed the document on the table. "We will destroy hundreds of American ships if they dare approach our islands—"

"We don't have the manpower to repel a true invasion," Kido interrupted.

"Wrong," Sato countered. "American troops have always outnumbered our troops on the occupied islands by two to one. But now it will be different. Our home army numbers in the hundreds of thousands, easily outnumbering the invasion force the Americans can throw at us. Our home army is well fed and well provisioned, unlike the occupied islands. And every Japanese man, woman, and child will fight with proud fanatical spirit. We *will* defend our islands. We *will* deal the Americans a mortal blow. They *will* have to sue for peace or lose a million of their sons trying."

Kido looked to Hiyakawa and finally grew silent. Both men understood the futility in further argument. They knew the war faction of the Cabinet would ultimately win out because there appeared no way to stop the military on their hellbent mission towards national suicide.

It was up to the Emperor now. Could he find the courage to stop them? Or would he yield to the unvoiced threat that always hung over the Imperial Chrysanthemum, that extremists would carry out a coup or foment other types of violence.

Kido and Hiyakawa feared the worst in their heart of hearts.

We Are Gods

"It's called the Thunder God Squadron," Jiro boasted enthusiastically as they arrived at the Kisarazu airbase near Tokyo.

To Connor, it didn't look like much or anything particularly different. Nothing like the naval airbase near Hiroshima where Fujiyama kept his private plane—a modified trainer—and where he taught Connor how to fly. Connor peered off to his left where, in a potato field, several Mitsubishi Zero fighter planes had been concealed by large, earth-colored tarps. The sight of these war machines caused his heart to race with anticipation, and he momentarily forgot the grave reason for his presence on the airfield.

"Come on. Let's sign in," Jiro said and pulled Connor forward.

As they arrived at a nondescript, semi-subterranean A-frame structure on the side of the field, they were joined by several other new recruits and an unpleasant surprise as well.

"*Goro*," Connor muttered under his breath.

When the Yakuza leader's eyes met Connor's, his face soured. "What are you doing here, ijin?" he snarled.

"He's here to protect his family," Jiro snapped in response. "To protect our country from atrocities and extinction at the hands of the Americans." Jiro stepped closer to Goro and jabbed a finger toward the man's chest. "Unlike you, who is only here for selfish glory."

This exchange was interrupted when an army officer entered the room and barked at the recruits, "Line up by that table."

The recruits followed suit and were faced with a simple slip of white paper when they reached the table. On the slip of paper, there were written three simple options: to *volunteer willingly*, to simply *volunteer*, or to *decline*.

"Choose one of the three," the officer ordered. "Sign your name at the top, and for those who agree to volunteer, move to the next room." He pointed to a door behind him.

As Connor and Jiro prepared to fill out the forms, Goro shoved himself between them and glared at Connor. He then withdrew a small sword from his belt and waved the blade in front of Connor's face.

Connor took a step back and watched as Goro pressed the razor-sharp point of the *wakizashi* and cut a slit in the center of his palm. He grabbed a fine brush that was used for signing the papers, dipped it in the blood that openly flowed from his palm, and signed his name. He grinned at Connor, seeming to challenge the American to do the same, then strode through the assigned door.

After Connor and Jiro signed their names under *volunteer willingly*, they joined the other pilots and pilots-to-be in a small conference room.

Army Air Force Captain, Mitsuzo Aramaki, entered the room and took center stage.

"Be seated," he ordered. He stood in front of the raw recruits with a blunt expression on his face, and looked in the eyes of every man, one-by-one, before addressing the room. "You are no longer sons, brothers, or fathers. From this moment forward, think of yourselves as bees. A swarm of bees that have a single-minded mission—to overcome the American carriers off our coast. Carriers that give the Americans air superiority over our country. But without that air superiority, these demons will think twice about invading our shores."

He continued to stare into the eyes before him, and his voice rose to a commanding tone. "You all must accept that bees die after they have stung. If you think like a bee, when you have eliminated all thoughts about life and death, you will be able to totally disregard your earthly life. This will also enable you to focus your attention on eradicating the enemy with unwavering determination." He paused, and his eyes locked momentarily on Connor's. "Your ultimate sacrifice will make you gods."

Connor glanced over at Jiro and noticed that he was nodding his head solemnly.

Aramaki allowed this to soak in for a moment, then continued. "The American carriers are anchored fifteen hundred miles from our islands at the Ulithi Atoll. The Americans are under the false belief that they are safe and unreachable. That will be their downfall. You pilots that stand before me, at this very moment, are Thunder Gods. You will gather together and form a mighty swarm of single-minded vengeance and honor. You will take to the skies, approach the American fleet and deliver a merciless attack."

Jiro nudged Connor and grinned. "We are Samurai. We are now living the Code."

Certain Kill

After the recruits were dismissed and handed their *tokkotai* pilot's manual, they were instructed to report to their quarters, compose their final will and testament, as well as a letter that would be delivered to their families after their mission had been completed.

"It states here," Jiro said as he flipped through the *tokkotai* pilot's manual, "that a pilot may return to base if they weren't successful in finding a suitable target. They are not to waste their life needlessly." He glanced up from the manual and stared at Connor. "But a pilot who continually returns to base will be executed after his ninth return."

Goro sat upon his bunk and scoffed at Connor's presence. "He should be shot if he ever returns. He is nothing but a coward!"

Connor ignored the remark, and Jiro shrugged off Goro's accusation as well and kept reading. "It says here that a pilot must never close his eyes. Never. Because if a pilot closes his eyes, he would lower the chances of hitting his target. In the final moments before the crash, the pilot is to scream *Hissatsu* at the top of his lungs."

"Certain kill", Goro muttered behind them.

A flight sergeant entered the quarters and announced, "Lights Out. Attack training starts at dawn."

Jiro leaned over to Connor and whispered, "We will do well tomorrow. Our destiny awaits us."

Death of a Samurai

Over the next several days, the men were subjected to grueling attack crash training maneuvers. The Mitsubishi Zero fighter planes would take off, immediately climb to 3,000 meters, dive to 1,500 meters, then ultimately plummet down to 200 meters before pulling up and touching down on the field. This routine was practiced time and again over the first few days until the pilots maneuvered their crafts with precision and without hesitation.

Then the next phase of the training commenced. It consisted of two types of attack: dive attack and the horizontal attack.

The recruits perched along the edge of the airfield as Captain Aramaki used his hands to demonstrate—one hand representing a ship and the other the crash fighter.

"In a body crash dive attack, you dive straight at the target and aim for a point between the bridge tower and the smoke stacks. Entering a smoke stack is also effective."

Aramaki affirmed the men understood his instruction before continuing on. "Now then, it is important that you do *not* aim at the enemy ship's bridge, tower or gun turret, but instead look for elevators or the flight deck itself to crash into. Understood?"

The young men nodded gravely.

Aramaki began to pace before his recruits. "For the horizontal attack, direct collision at the middle of the ship, slightly higher than the waterline, or if you're not able to accomplish that, aim at the entrance to the aircraft hangar, or the bottom of the stack."

The recruits nodded in unison again.

"On a mission," the Captain continued, "you will fly in formation to the target area then break up so each of you can find your own target and dive into it. If the formation is attacked by enemy fighters before we reach the target area, scatter in different directions in order to avoid multiple losses to our ranks, then *if* you survive, simply fall back into formation and resume attack to the targeted areas."

Connor quickly raised his hand. "But isn't it guaranteed the enemy will send up fighters?"

"Hai. That is why we take off at night and approach the target area in the cover of darkness, then attack our targets at the crack of dawn when they become visible."

Aramaki looked to the other recruit and continued. "Understand that some of you will also fly as escorts to divert enemy fighters from the attacking planes and after completing that task, you will report back on the mission."

Aramaki stopped pacing and clapped his hands together. "Oi. Now let's do the drill."

The recruits stood and started to make their way toward the planes. Connor watched as Aramaki pulled Jiro aside and seemed to speak to him in a stern fashion.

After a few moments, Jiro nodded and bowed as Aramaki turned and marched toward the planes. When Jiro shuffled over to Connor, he was nearly in tears. "I won't be permitted to fly any missions."

Connor asked why even though he knew the answer.

"I've damaged two planes while attempting landings. Jiro hung his head in shame and choked back stubborn tears.

Connor placed his hand on Jiro's shoulder to comfort him when the scream of the air raid alarms pierced the air.

"Everyone to the shelters!" Aramaki ordered.

The recruits turned and looked up at a formation of B-29 bombers roaring over their heads, being escorted by a flight of P-51 Mustangs.

As the men ran to the safety of the shelter, two of the Mustangs peeled off and dived directly towards the airfield, peppering the tarmac with machine gun and canon fire.

As Connor stumbled into the safety of a bunker, he searched for Jiro. "Where's Jiro?"

Goro stared out the bunker and pointed to the potato field. Jiro was sprinting toward one of the Zeros.

"What is he doing?" Connor screamed. His answer came a few moments later.

Upon reaching the plane, Jiro climbed aboard and started the engine. A moment later, he turned the plane towards the airfield and began to accelerate his Zero down the runway.

The P-51s rumbled around for another pass, but by then, Jiro's plane was in the air and climbing past the diving Mustangs, headed straight up with his target in sight—the B-29s.

Jiro focused his sites on one of the bombers bringing up the rear of the formation, and as Connor and the others watched from outside the shelter, he closed in on the American plane.

Jiro flew closer and closer to his target as those on the ground watched him slam his plane into the belly of the B29, instantly incinerating both himself and the bomber in a massive ball of fire.

As fiery chunks of the Zero and bomber plummeted to the ground, Connor and the other pilots stood in stunned silence.

No one spoke until Aramaki nodded at the flaming wreckage. "He died a Samurai."

Suki Surprise

"Who are *they*?" a pilot recruit asked and pointed out the window toward a long line of young women walking upon the air base.

Connor rolled out of his bunk and peered outside. "I don't know…" His words trailed off, and he made an immediate beeline out of the barracks and onto the airfield. He jogged passed the line of young Japanese women until he reached one in particular. He touched the woman on the shoulder, and as she turned to face him, a broad smile spread over her face.

It was Suki.

"Connor-san?!" she gasped.

After they quickly embraced, Connor pulled back and stared at his sister. "What are you doing here?"

"What else? I came to help," she replied and waved to the young girls around her. "We're *all* here to help," waving her hand over."

"But…"

"Mama-san told me what you said to her, Connor-san. She knew what you were going to do. So I contacted Hiryo at his airbase, knowing he was training special attack pilots, and he tracked you down here." She looked up at Connor with doleful eyes. "Aren't you glad to see me?"

Connor smiled and gave her another tight hug. "Of course."

She smiled bittersweet at Connor's inability of masking his sadness. "I know the promise you made my father. I know what the Americans have done to our innocents." Tears welled up in her eyes. "Aiko and now Kenji. If we don't stop the Americans in any way possible, they will reduce our homes and cities to ashes."

She took Connor's hand in hers and squeezed gently. "Gyokusai, fighting to the death of the people, is now a reality, not just a slogan anymore." She wiped the tears from her eyes. "You are Japanese, Connor-san. More so than you know."

Dishonored

Over the next few days, as Suki and the other Japanese women took care of the recruits' needs—cooking, mending, laundering, and cleaning their quarters—the time came for the pilots to do what they had been trained to do. To attack and sink the carriers of an American enemy task force southeast of Tokyo.

As the sun set, some of the pilots finished their wills while others wrote poems. Connor presented Suki with a box of his hair and fingernail clippings so there would be something of him left to cremate. In return, Suki placed a floating chrysanthemum over his silk scarf and under his leather helmet and goggles.

Cherry blossoms and small dolls were given to each of the pilots as tokens of love and support. One item was placed in the cockpit of their plane, and the other hung from the flight clock.

As darkness fell upon the airfield, Suki followed Connor and the others to the side of the runway where a small table stood next to a little shrine. On the table sat ceremonial cups of sake. "Japan is strong," the young girls in attendance offered as pilots consumed their ritualistic drink.

At his request, Connor was permitted to carry the ashes of Jiro inside his air suit.

Aramaki approached his men and saluted them firmly. "Pilots! Man your planes."

Goro suddenly fell out of line and pointed toward Connor. "He should not be permitted to go. He is a coward and does not deserve the glory of the kamikaze. He refused to kill a traitor to our country."

Captain Aramaki turned and glared at Goro. "What are you talking about?"

"He was ordered to kill a traitor. And he refused," Goro then informed the Captain of Connor's refusal to kill Fujiyama on the Yakazu raid of his house.

Aramaki approached Connor. "Is this true?"

Connor nodded his head firmly. "Hai. He told me to kill my father, but my father was no traitor."

Aramaki mulled this over for several moments before making his decision. "You will fly as escort for the mission."

Connor's stomach lurched. But before Connor could argue, Aramaki addressed his pilots. "Man your planes!"

Connor peered over to Suki, who gave him an encouraging nod, then made his way despondently to his Zero.

The pilots started the engines of their Zeros, and the planes roared off one-by-one into the setting sun, their engines barking as they rose from the tarmac. Once airborne, the two-dozen planes fell into formation above the airfield, then turned southeast and headed in the direction of the ocean.

As the formation flew through the night, a full moon rose to replace a setting sun. As he approached the coast, Connor, deep in his thoughts and once again feeling betrayed, suddenly felt his Zero shudder violently.

He looked over his shoulder and saw another Zero firing at him. *Goro!*

Connor weaved his fighter left and right, trying to avoid the lethal spray of machine gun fire from Goro's plane when a crackling voice came over his intercom.

"They will know you died a coward!" Goro screamed. "You will die with no honor, ijin!"

Connor attempted to evade Goro's torrent of fire, but it was no use. His plane's engine started to smoke, then sputter.

The firing abruptly ceased, and in the pale cast of moonlight, he saw Goro turning in for the kill. He came straight at Connor, guns focused on his adversary.

Connor attempted to fire his machine guns to defend himself, but they had been disabled by Goro's attack. He could only watch and wait for Goro to end his life.

Suddenly, Goro's plane exploded in a blazing ball of flame directly in front of him.

Flying through the flaming remains of Goro's plane, and pulling straight up in front of Connor doing a barrel roll of victory, flew a U.S. Navy Corsair.

Connor's exuberant mood lasted only a second. His engine shuddered and went dead, sending his Zero into a dive. He fought with the controls, desperately trying to keep the Zero in the air as long as possible, when he spotted a wide rice paddy below.

He guided the Zero the best he could towards the soft landing, pressed his eyes closed, and braced for the impact.

Alienation Complete

Connor dreamed of his Japanese family, all together in their tranquil home, eating breakfast, chatting and laughing and enjoying one another's easy company. It was a safe place. A real home that embodied love and security. It was nice to be back.

Then he awoke.

He peered out the cracked window of his Zero, black smoke swirling all around him. He quickly unbuckled his harness, clambered out of his wrecked plane and tumbled into the muddied waters of the rice paddy. He tried to stand, but a wave of vertigo overcame him, and he collapsed on the bank of the paddy field.

Workers, having witnessed the fighter's crash landing, approached Connor with deliberate hesitation. They chattered amongst themselves in puzzled Japanese, not quite able to make sense of an American climbing out of a downed Zero.

Connor neither had the will nor energy to explain himself, so he mustered his last bit of remaining strength and hobbled as quickly as he could away from the scene. His mind stood muddled in a haze not only from the scrapes and cuts across his body, but also from what had just transpired. His thoughts and emotions were in a state of jumbled chaos. American and Japanese memories cascaded upon each other, sending his mind reeling with more and more turmoil. Nothing made sense anymore. Nothing. He had been rejected as an American and almost killed because he was Japanese—from the very people he wanted most to be accepted by.

His utter alienation stood complete. Alienated from his family, his friends, and his adopted society at large. Everywhere he turned to discover who he really was—to become a true Samurai, to truly live the code, *to know himself*—had been unilaterally blocked.

As these thoughts reared their ugly truths, two realizations flashed in his mind at once: *Nurikabe and Nakamura.*

Miyoko had told him that he would someday find a way around his Nurikabe, that which was blocking his path, and recalled what Nakamura had said many months ago.

A Samurai must know oneself, not lose oneself.

He knew at that moment that he had to find Nakamura. In Connor's mind, he was the only one that could help lift the pain of his alienation.

He finally slowed his pace and dropped to his knees, water soaking through his tattered uniform. Through stinging tears, he glimpsed a smoldering city many miles in the distance. He knew it to be Tokyo. Bombed and ravaged into near oblivion.

Connor vowed to himself that once he got his bearings, he would seek out Nakamura at the Buddhist Temple.

On the outskirts of the devastated city, walking through the sweltering heat of the remains of July, 1945, Connor witnessed the horror of what the Americans had done to one of the world's greatest metropolis. The smell of charred wood and debris clung to the air even from that distance.

As he walked the streets of the suburb, lined with scorched homes, he noticed a small group of women and children foraging through a downed B-29 for scraps of metal—metal needed for the war effort.

He continued on down a small street and came upon a group of people standing around a boy lying in the gutter. He looked to be a teenager, close to Connor's age, but he could have been older. He looked so emaciated. It was obvious that the boy was dying of starvation.

The group of survivors didn't notice Connor—all the better as he watched the boy draw his last remaining breathe. After the boy grew still, an old man came and spread a straw mat over the body as the boiling summer sun beat down on the corpse.

He was an unknown boy dying on an unknown street, and the symbolism was not lost on Connor.

Connor averted his eyes and continued on his quest.

Soon he came to a railroad station and was surprised to see that one of the trains was still operating. He walked towards the station, and his attention was drawn to a child who had just fallen from his bike. Instinctively, Connor went to the small boy, picked him off the ground, and noticed that he was bleeding.

"Are you alright?"

But before he could answer, the boy's parents rushed up and snatched the boy from Connor's grasp, hatred burning in their eyes.

Connor offered no resistance. He simply backed away and walked up to the station platform and boarded the waiting train. He studied the route map in the car and saw that it went to the station he and Aiko had stopped at to go to the Buddhist Temple.

As the train lurched from the station, his mind drifted to his recent experiences which proved to only deepened his demoralized mood.

Truth

"Who are you?" the small Buddhist monk inquired warily.

"My name is Connor Fujiyama, and I must speak with Nakamura."

The little monk studied Connor's face, his tattered uniform, and the cuts and bruises upon his arms as he considered the request.

"Nakamura knows me," Connor urged. "We met before and spoke several months ago."

After what felt like an eternity to Connor, the monk seemed to finally make a decision. "Come with me."

Connor followed the monk to a small room, opened the door, and motioned for him to enter.

Connor complied and saw Nakamura sitting on the tile floor behind a small wood desk. The afternoon sunlight streamed in from windows and reflected off the top of Nakamura's bald head.

"Nakamura-san," Connor whispered in a low voice in keeping with the tranquil atmosphere.

Nakamura turned from copying his sutras. "Connor-san. I'm pleased to see you again."

Connor bowed quickly and wasted no time. "I need your help. I didn't know who else to turn to."

"Come. Have tea with me."

"But there's no time—"

"Tea first. Then talk," Nakamura coaxed.

Connor conceded and followed Nakamura in silence back to his quarters. Connor maintained his silence as Nakamura meticulously prepared tea and then poured a cup for he and his guest.

"Now. Tell me? What has you so deeply troubled?"

And, as if a damn had been breached, Connor confessed to the warrior monk everything that had transpired since he met with him months ago, and that everywhere he turned his way was blocked.

"Nurikabe," Nakamura mused.

"Hai," Connor replied, then hung his head. "I don't know what to do. I don't know how to get through it. The final—Nurikabe—was the betrayal at the hands of another kamikaze."

Nakamura slowly nodded. "Hai. Betrayal is rampant in our country. Betrayal of the militarists and their warped version of the Samurai code." He sipped his tea and put down the cup. "So you thought that becoming a kamikaze—sacrificing oneself—was the code of the Samurai, and you could redeem yourself?"

"Isn't that the code?" Connor pressed. "To sacrifice oneself?"

"The Samurai code is not to die needlessly."

"But what about honor?"

"Dying needlessly is not honor. What does that prove? Who exactly does that honor?"

Connor was unable to directly answer the question. "There is no real code. No one can be trusted. There is bigotry and hypocrisy on both sides—American and Japanese. Both are unjust and unable to provide justice. There is no hope. No purpose. No truth."

Nakamura placed his hand on the troubled boy's shoulder. "Truth? You want to know what is truth?"

Connor lifted his head and wiped his eyes. "Hai. I do."

Nakamura poured himself another cup of tea and proceeded to tell a story. "Once upon a time, a King decided to make his people tell the truth. He believed he could force his kingdom to practice truthfulness. He decided to build a gallows on the bridge entering his city and question each person who entered. The very next day, when the gates were opened at dawn, the Captain of the Guard was stationed with a squad of troops to question all that entered.

The King then pronounced, *Everyone will be questioned. If he tells the truth, he will be allowed to enter. If he lies, he will be hanged on the gallows.*"

He paused a moment, then went on. "One day, a traveler, a local wise man, approached the gates of the city. The Captain of the Guard commanded, *Stop! Where are you going?*

"*I am on my way to be hanged*, said the wise man.

"*I don't believe you!* the Captain said.

"*Very well, if I have told a lie, then hang me!* replied the wise man."

"The Captain was stopped by this remark and said, *But if we hang you for lying, we will have made what you said come true!*

"*That's right*, said the wise man. *Now you know what truth is: YOUR truth!*"

Nakamura placed his hands upon his lap. "Connor-san, you will have to find *your* truth. You will have to find your own meaning—your own purpose. You must empower yourself and not seek empowerment from others. You will have to find who you are. Not to lose yourself in what others tell you what you are."

Connor nodded, trying to process the moral of the story and the monk's wisdom.

"Try to be the best of both Japanese and American and forge your own purpose. Your own destiny." He held Connor's hand. "Return home. The war will be over soon, and the people will have to bear the unbearable. Your mother and sister will need you."

Unexpected Cellmate

Hours turned to days, every breathing moment proving to be unbearable in my dark and dank prison of the Hiroshima Kempeitai headquarters. The daylight hours were long and torturous with nothing to do or occupy my mind, and nighttime provided little relief as I tossed and turned, trying to find escape and comfort from the fleas that infested my bed and attacked my body mercilessly.

But then, on August 5th, I received an unexpected cellmate. I assumed Major Takahashi, in a perverted sense of humor, felt I would be more *comfortable* with my own kind.

"Williams," the stranger said, extending his hand and introducing himself. Part of his cheek was gone; only a sunken hole of tattered flesh remained.

I knew at once that the man was an American POW.

Quite frankly relieved to have any kind of company, I made an effort to make small talk. "Where were you captured?"

Williams stood tall and gaunt from the ravages of war and incarceration, but his blue eyes still sparkled with cruel vitality. "In the Philippines. When they fell to the Japs. After a year or so they put us on work crews then shipped a bunch of us up to a Tokyo prison." He searched his pockets for a cigarette. "Had it good there. Even my love life," he smirked as he thought about Barbara Hiyakawa. "Then they shipped me here for some kind of *indiscretion* I committed."

His grin transformed into an ugly sneer. "You a Jap?"

"American. Japanese-American." Then I added, "And I'm to be shot as a traitor."

That fact seemed to satisfy Williams. "Filthy Japs. Serves you right."

Just then, the cellblock opened and Takahashi walked up and peered through the bars to my cell. "Enjoying your company?" he asked sarcastically. "Rats like the company of their own."

I walked up to my cell bars and attempted to present a brave front. "So, when is my execution?"

"Soon. Very soon. As will all traitors like you who want Japan to be defeated or surrender." He brought his face up close to mine —I could smell the sake on his breath—and said mysteriously, "*All* traitors."

A Frightening Threat

The next morning, Takahashi made an appearance at the Fuji-yama home, dressed in full regalia, with the intention of demanding Suki's hand in marriage. He entered the house as if he lived there, and his presence clearly caused Miyoko and Suki discomfort.

"I am a hero of the nation," he bragged to Suki as he stood in the kitchen and pointed to the medals pinned to his chest.

Suki eyed Takahashi's medals and shook her head in disgust. "Is that for the many people you've killed?"

Miyoko, standing beside her daughter, could see that Takahashi was not pleased with Suki's retort. He dismissed the snide remark and bragged of the one hundred heads he had decapitated from the enemy.

Suki was visibly shaken at his sickening narrative. "I would never *think* of marrying a man like you. Never!"

"You are a Japanese woman," he barked. "You have no mind of your own to think and will do as you are told!"

When Suki opened her mouth to respond, Takahashi's hand flashed forward, hitting her across the face so violently it drove her to floor. "Silence! Keep your mouth shut."

"Leave her alone!" Miyoko screamed. When she stepped in front of her daughter, Takahashi reared back and punched her square in the face.

Miyoko dropped to the floor next to her daughter.

Suki watched in horror as blood trickled from her mother's mouth. "You're an animal!" she screamed.

Takahashi glared down at the both of them and jabbed his finger toward their faces. "This traitorous family will pay. All those who oppose the war will pay. All pacifists will pay. A new order is coming! *Kyūjō*!" he shouted.

With that, he spit directly in their faces and stormed out of the house.

"What does he mean by that?" Miyoko managed to choke out.

Suki shook her head. "I don't know. But he's threatened our family. He is capable of anything."

Rumors

It was a sunny, cloudless early morning in Hiroshima, so clear you could see for miles into the pure blue sky. But not even the pleasant morning could lift the spirits that plagued Suki with helpless anxiety and fear.

She walked amongst the city's citizens, including numerous schoolchildren, recruited to prepare for future bombings by tearing down entire houses in order to create fire lanes.

Up to that point, the city had been largely spared the rain of air bombing that had ravaged so many other Japanese cities. Rumors abounded as to why this was so, from the fact that many Hiroshima residents had emigrated from America, to the supposed presence of President Truman's mother in the area as well.

Just as she reached the train station, at around 7 AM, air raid alarms screeched throughout the city. All eyes peered to the sky to spot a lone silver plane approaching the metropolis.

But the plane's presence didn't seem to bother many of the people—they were accustomed to seeing lone B-29s fly over the city sky. In fact, they were told that they were merely reconnaissance planes, so the citizens went back to their morning routines.

They, and the world itself, were not prepared for what came next.

And the World Stopped

As the lone B-29 trailed off into the sky, Suki boarded the train to the Kanoya Naval Base and to Hiryo. She felt, somehow, he could protect their family. The journey proved to be slow and tedious. Every dozen miles or so, the train had to switch tracks due to bombing damage and was forced to take detours. After an hour of monotonous traveling, Suki was no more than ten miles from the city.

As the train made its slow voyage away from Hiroshima, Suki looked out her window at the rolling landscape. Thoughts of Takahashi's threats on her family weighed heavily upon her mind.

At that instant, a sudden burst of searing bright light appeared on her left in the distance. All of the other passengers near her saw the same thing as well.

Then abruptly, a tremendous force jerked the entire train and shook it from end to end. People screamed in terror and luggage from the racks above came hurdling down on top of them.

Suki felt an intense wave of stifling heat in the car that dissipated quickly. She regained her balance, and she and the other passengers quickly exited the train and scrambled toward a nearby cabbage field. From there, Suki glimpsed something she had never witnessed before.

A vertical column of brownish bile boiled and bubbled up in rainbow hues of purples, oranges, and reds over the city of Hiroshima. The intense, angry cloud appeared mesmerizing, breathtaking and ominous all at the same time.

Suki's thoughts immediately turned to her mother. She knew she must go back to the city no matter what the cost might be.

A Prediction Filled

It was sudden and dreamlike. The floor of my cell buckled and thrust up below my feet. My cellmate, Williams, felt it, too. How could he not?

My initial thought was that an earthquake, common for Japan, had just occurred. But what followed next drove that possibility from my mind. A tremendous, deafening blast tore through the entire jail. Chunks of rock, wood, and other building materials flew in every direction. I buried my body, or as much as I could manage, under my bunk, shielding me from most of the debris. When the shaking ceased, I looked above my head to see the entire building above me had been blown away.

Then came the searing heat.

My cell transformed into an oven as an invisible heat wave tore above through what was left of the Kempeitai Hiroshima head-quarters. I scrambled to my feet, and as I surveyed this startling scene, I gazed up at the open sky and saw a mushroom cloud rapidly rising in the sky several miles from my cell. The deadly cloud was spreading and expanding quickly, completely blotting out the morning sun.

Williams and I stumbled out of our basement confinement and towards the street where we were faced with a horror unseen in our worst nightmares.

Hiroshima had disappeared. The city had simply ceased to exist.

"What the hell happened?" Williams shouted.

"I don't know," I replied. "Some kind of an explosion."

Then I recalled what Hiyakawa told me about the monk's prediction and uttered aloud, "*A weapon, so powerful, that it could destroy an entire city all at once. A weapon so fierce, it would change the course of history and create an era of fear of the total destruction of civilization.*"

Williams stared at me as if I had gone crazy.

"A prediction," I whispered.

"By who?"

"A Buddhist monk. It seems he wasn't mad at all."

"Well, screw him and his prediction," Williams replied as he looked at the devastation. "We need to get away from here as fast as possible."

For once, I had to agree with the American POW.

A Horrible Pilgrimage

After a grueling three hours of fearing the worst, Suki finally made it to the city. Once there, she was greeted with a grim reality: Hiroshima had been transformed into a gigantic inferno. Fires erupted everywhere. It seemed as if the earth itself emitted fire and smoke with flames erupting from the exposed earth. The sky stood saddled with darkness, the ground was scarlet, and in between hung clouds of yellowish smoke.

Nothing remained of the city except a few random buildings that had been reinforced with concrete. As far as Suki's eyes could see, the city lay before her like a desert dotted with piles of brick and roofing tile. It was not like the destruction she had seen in Tokyo. No. This was total *devastation*.

The peculiar odor of burning human flesh surrounded her and inundated her nostrils. Zombie-like men, women, and children stumbled in all directions, begging for water. They stood naked, with horrific burns, their clothing ripped from their bodies.

Suki felt repulsed and sickened by the sight of strips of skin dangling from their bodies, walking with arms extended to avoid touching their own flesh. Adding to the ghastly spectacle were the pathetic sounds coming from the victims horrible groans and cries as if they had traveled from the very depths of hell.

Victims had no hair, burned completely off their scalps, and at a glance, she couldn't tell whether she was looking at them from the front or the back.

They appeared as living ghosts and not like people of this world. A young girl, twelve or thirteen, stumbled aimlessly amongst the ashes at her feet. She dropped to the ground in what she thought was a puddle of water. "Water! Water!" she cried.

As she scooped the festering liquid to her lips, her skin bubbled and dissolved into gelatinous flesh.

Suki turned away and soon reached a bridge on the way to her home. From there she saw that the entire Hiroshima Castle had been completely leveled to the ground. The bridge itself smoldered under her feet, and she watched as bloated corpses floated in the moat like trash.

Some of the living approached Suki, pleading for a drink of water. Many were blinded, with blackened pockets of flesh for eyes. Other had blood gushing from their mouths and ears, their faces unrecognizable.

It was if the worlds of the living and the dead had converged. If there was a hell, Suki was in the middle of it.

Despite the horror that stood all around her, Suki's only thought was to find her mother.

Justice

As Williams and I, two unlikely traveling companions, walked through the devastation that was once a beautiful, vibrant city, my thoughts went to Fujiyama's family.

Did they survive? Did they need help?

I stopped at a street intersection that I thought I recognized and looked to Williams. "I'm going this way," I said and pointed in the direction of the Fujiyama home.

"Um... I'll come with you."

Through his tough, brazen exterior, I could see that Williams was becoming increasingly nervous walking around as an American. I guess he assumed that being with a Japanese person might protect him from the people's disdain and outrage—or worse.

Eventually I found the general area of the Fujiyama home. The entire area had been demolished. I could feel Williams watch me as I scanned the neighborhood.

"What are you looking for?"

"A house."

"A house? There's nothing here but debris," he snapped.

"Let's keep moving."

We started to walk again when suddenly I heard my name ring out. "Yoshihara!"

I turned as Suki threw herself into my arms.

"It's gone," she sobbed into my chest. "Mother is gone. The house—everything! It's all gone."

I held her to my chest and let her cry out her pain and despair. Then, finally, she peered into my eyes. "Please. Help me find my mother," she begged.

I nodded and assured her that I would. I pointed toward the street behind us. "Is that your street?"

"Hai."

"I'll go down that way, and you go in the other direction."

The two of us split up. Williams was the last thing on my mind.

I began the horrific chore of sifting through the debris of several homes and discovered numerous crushed bodies—the remains of families that were busy having breakfast that bright and sunny morning, families that had no inkling of the horror that was about to befall them. I kept at the grizzly task hoping against hope. Hoping that Suki and I might find her mother.

Then I heard a scream—a woman's terrified scream. I looked up the street and heard it again.

I ran towards the cry of distress and discovered Williams holding Suki by the throat. Her clothing had been ripped off her body, exposing her breasts and genitals.

"Scream again and I'll kill you," Williams snarled.

"Williams! I ordered. "Let her go!"

Williams turned and stared at me with eyes void of reason and compassion. Then he smiled as he dropped Suki to the dirt where she cried and gasped for air.

"What do you care? She's just another dirty, Jap whore."

"*You-are-a-fucking-animal*," I hissed. "Just like the ones that destroyed this city."

Williams barely flinched and maintained his devilish grin. "OK. OK. You win." He grabbed Suki by the arm, yanked her up violently, then shoved her towards me. As I reached to catch her, out of the corner of my eyes, I watched Williams rear back and swing a plank of charred wood towards my head. I fell to the ground.

"Now," Williams sneered, as he stood over the prostrate Suki. "Where were we?"

Suki's only response was to hold her hands in front of her face and sob uncontrollably.

"I'll give you something to cry about." He yanked her up by a clump of hair and dragged her over to a smooth piece of rock. As he tossed her over the stone, the surface bit into Suki's naked back. He bent over, spread her legs wide and pressed the full weight of his frame against hers. When she tried to claw at his face, he snatched her hands and pinned them above her head. "Now, you Jap whore, you ready to surrender?"

"No," ordered a voice from behind him. "You surrender. You son-of-a-bitch."

Williams glanced over his shoulder just as Connor slammed a chunk of heavy stone against the side of his head. The POW's body immediately went limp, and he collapsed on top of Suki.

Connor quickly rolled his father off of Suki and helped her to her feet. "Are you okay?"

"You're *alive*," she gasped with tears streaking down her face. "But I saw you fly off on the mission."

Before he could respond, Suki's eyes went wide and she screamed in alarm.

Connor turned to see his enraged father grasping a long sharp pole over his head.

"Die, you filthy bitch!" Williams snarled.

Connor had little time to react. He instinctively threw his body in front of Suki to shield her from the coming blow. He felt his ribs crack, and he dropped to the pavement, writhing in agony.

He waited for the assault to continue when he heard a scuffling from behind him. He peered up and watched a handful of Japanese men beating Williams with sticks and large rocks. As they bludgeoned his body, they cursed him, vowing revenge for the destruction of their city by the Americans.

Williams' high-pitched shrieks echoed down the street as his body was pummeled and broken by the angry mob.

Suki covered her exposed body with her hands and averted her eyes at the terrible spectacle. But Connor did not. He watched stoically as the mob continued to beat on his father's bloody, lifeless corpse.

"Justice," Connor whispered. "Justice."

Kyūjō

That night, I found myself sitting with Connor and Suki, eating a sparse dinner in some refugee center miles from the city. Though Suki was still shaken and traumatized by the incident with Williams and the devastation of Hiroshima, she asked why I had been in prison.

I explained that I had uncovered the truth about Unit 731 and how the Kempeitai found out about my report which resulted in the execution of my editor and my own death sentence.

We continued to talk into the night, both Suki and I rapt with fascination by Connor's admission of joining the kamikaze ranks. Our conversation turned to the how Takahashi had threatened Suki's family. "He mentioned a word—one that I didn't understand," she admitted.

"What word?" I asked.

"*Kyūjō.* Do you know what it means?"

"Hai. It means a wrestler's absence from a honbasho, usually due to injury. The point being his absence from continuing an activity." I thought on this for a moment. "I saw many troops of the Kwantung Army in Tokyo and Hiroshima. They shouldn't be in the home islands. And if *Kyūjō* is a reference to the Emperor, his absence from continuing the war..."

"A coup?" Suki interjected. "To overthrow the Emperor?"

"I'm afraid so." I stood up on weary legs. "We have to warn the Palace."

"And how are we suppose to do that?" Connor asked. "If you're right about the Kwantung troops, how are we going to get to anyone in the Palace?"

"Perhaps we can try and get to my brother," Suki suggested.

"No. No time," I replied. "Besides that, we can't trust anyone around your brother. We don't know how deep this conspiracy runs."

"I know someone we can trust," Connor said quietly. "Some one that can get us in the Palace. Even to the Emperor."

Suki and I stared at him, our faces twisted into confusion.

Who could Connor possibly know who could gain access into the palace?

To Treat with Silent Contempt

Hiyakawa and Lord Kido gathered in the office of the Keeper of the Privy Seal of Japan and read over the reports coming out of Hiroshima. The two men were as confused as the reports themselves, but one thing was certain. The Americans had vowed to utilize a new kind of weapon at the Potsdam Conference held recently in Germany, and it seemed their threats were to be taken very seriously.

Hiyakawa read aloud a copy of a leaflet that B-29s had begun dropping on Tokyo.

Because your military leaders have rejected the 13-part surrender declaration, we have employed our atomic bomb. Before we use this bomb again and again to destroy every resource of your military by which they are prolonging this useless war, petition the Emperor now to end the war.

Hiyakawa glanced up from the leaflet. "Unconditional surrender. If these reports out of Hiroshima are even remotely accurate, the Emperor must consider it." He leaned closer to Kido. "What has the Cabinet decided?"

"*Mokusatsu,*" Kido replied solemnly. "Nothing. *To treat the Allies' demands with silent contempt.*" He shook his head before continuing. "In confidence, the Cabinet is seeking a peace deal in which to avoid any Allied occupation of the home islands, retain the inner empire, retain the Emperor, repatriate our troops, *and* avoid any Allied war crimes trials."

Hiyakawa laughed bitterly. "Too much. I don't believe the Allies will concede. The Emperor must force a surrender."

Kido stared directly at Hiyakawa. "Dangerous. Very dangerous. To do that, he would have to defy the military. A call for peace would almost certainly put the Chrysanthemum throne in danger." He sighed. "The Emperor has called for a meeting. He will demand a decision today. Bring whatever materials you have and meet me at the Palace."

Disgraced Samurai

On August 8th, after a long, grueling journey by train, Connor, Suki, and I finally arrived at a Buddhist Temple outside of Tokyo. We had traveled by train mostly at night. The trip was slowed both by detours past damaged rail lines and from American fighter planes seeking out targets of opportunity, such as trains, during the daylight hours.

During the journey, Connor told us of Nakamura and why he thought the man would be of help to us.

Upon our arrival that August night, the monks said very little, merely showed us to our quarters and informed us that Nakamura would meet with us in the morning.

Early the next morning, we gathered to meet with Nakamura, who sat drinking tea in his quarters, and before we had the chance to tell him of our news, he spoke solemnly.

"Nagasaki has been destroyed," he stated, shaking his head. "Most of the city is gone. Nearly 100,000 dead."

"Just like Hiroshima?" I asked.

"Hai. It looks like the very same weapon was used." He peered past us and stared out his window. "I fear the Americans will turn our cities into dust. The Emperor *must* press the Cabinet to offer peace."

"Nakamura," Connor interrupted. "That is why we are here. We need you help." He went on to explain our concerns about a military coup and the pressing need to reach someone in the Palace to warn the Emperor on these matters.

Nakamura's answer to our request for help was swift.

"No."

"*No?*" Connor asked, stupefied. "But why?"

"Because I would be of no help," he replied apologetically.

"I don't understand," Connor replied. "You're a hero of the country and can request an audience with the Emperor."

"The Emperor will not wish to see a disgraced hero." He stared into his tea as if glimpsing into the past.

"Disgraced?" I asked. "You said you were honored by the Emperor for your naval service. You said you came from a long line of Samurai," Connor argued.

"That's true. A *disgraced* line of Samurai."

The three of us stood silent and waited for him to continue.

He swirled his tea a few times and finally spoke. "I was forced out of the Imperial Navy due to my family's dishonor." He peered directly at Connor. "Remember the discussion we had of the 47 Ronin? Remember how they lost all honor with their revenge on the enemy Lord?"

"So?" Connor replied.

"My family line descends directly from one of those 47 Ronin," he whispered. "When certain political factions in the government saw how close I had become to Emperor Hirohito's father, Emperor Taishō, they exposed my family line. I instantly became disgraced, and the Emperor had no choice but to disavow me." He waved his hand around him. "I left public life, came to this temple, and remained here ever since."

"But how do you know the emperor will not see you now?" Connor countered. "He knows of your heroism in the war against Russia?"

"Hai. But he also knows of my disgrace. That remains, and nothing can change that. He would never see me."

A Precedent

Shortly before midnight, Hiyakawa joined Kido at the Cabinet meeting with Hirohito in a hot, humid air-raid shelter sixty feet below the Imperial Library.

The Emperor, looking weary and broken, sat in a straight-backed chair and wore a field marshal's uniform. The regal costume was ill fitting, as tailors were not allowed to touch this man revered as a god.

Hirohito sat impatiently, listening as each cabinet member presented his argument.

At 2 a.m. on Friday, August 10th, Prime Minister Kantaro Suzuki did something that no prime minister had ever done before. He stood from his chair and directly addressed the Emperor. "Your Highness. We request an Imperial Command. A Voice of the Crane."

Everyone present knew exactly what that meant. The sacred bird could be heard even when it flew unseen.

The room fell silent awaiting Hirohito's response. When he did, he spoke softly, barely audible. "I do not believe that our nation can continue to fight a war. The time has come when we must bear the insufferable. I swallow my own tears and pride, and give my sanction to the proposal to accept the Allied Potsdam proclamation."

With that, the Emperor stood up and quietly exited the shelter.

Prime Minister Suzuki turned and addressed the Foreign Ministers. "Transmit to the Allies our offer to accept the terms of the Potsdam Declaration, but with this nonnegotiable understanding."

With emphasis he declared, "The Emperor must *not* be removed from the throne."

A Chance at Redemption

Asmall, soft-talking monk entered Connor's room in the middle of the night and whispered softly. "Awaken, sir. Come with me."

The little monk led Connor to a small garden near their quarters. There in a meditative position in the center of a Zen garden sat Nakamura. He gazed up and signaled for Connor to approach.

Connor nodded and sat on a small wooden bench by the warrior monk.

"I know you are filled with disappointment in me, Connor-san. But there is little I can do."

Connor did not argue that point. "You speak of honor and loyalty, yet you would let the Emperor possibly be deposed. We need to try and stop it. *You* need to try. We can't allow those who brought so much pain and suffering to me, my family, and all the other families across this country to continue this war."

Connor's body trembled as he stood up and looked down at the warrior monk. "I was willing to sacrifice my life to protect my family, to take them out of harm's way. And I'm prepared to do so again. We need to try anything in our power to warn him. And it is your responsibility as well. Otherwise, the blood of thousands, possibly millions, will be on your hands."

"The effort would be useless," Nakamura replied. "Besides that, it is no longer my responsibility."

Connor's voice rose and pierced the tranquil air of the Zen garden. "It's the responsibility of *your* generation. You yourself told me of its betrayal. Of how it betrayed the country. Now, here at this moment, is your chance to redeem your entire generation."

Connor waited for Nakamura's response. Finally, the warrior monk responded.

"You would make a very good Samurai, Connor-san. You have learned Makato."

"And why is that?" Connor asked with an unsteady voice.

"When a Samurai says that they will perform an action, it is as good as done. Nothing will stop them from completing what they say they will do. You are Samurai. You have proven that."

Nakamura stood and placed his hand upon Connor's shoulder. "Today we go to Tokyo."

A Chance

That very same evening, we arrived in Tokyo at a small family restaurant located near the Palace. Nakamura knew the owners well and was assured that they would ask no questions. Especially questions about Connor's presence.

"Kon'nichiwa, Tomika-san," Nakamura said to a short, lean man wearing a soiled apron.

"Kon'nichiwa," Tomika replied.

"These are my friends," Nakamura said, pointing to us one-by-one. "Please share with them your hospitality."

"Hai," Tomika replied without question.

Nakamura turned to us. "Wait here. I will attempt to reach Hiyakawa and hope he will meet with us."

As Nakamura left the restaurant, Tomika extended his arms towards the dining area. "Please. Have some food."

He didn't have to ask twice.

Voice of the Crane

"Come with me," Kido instructed Hiyakawa. "The Emperor declared another *gozen kaigin*. He has issued an Imperial command for the Cabinet to prepare an Imperial rescript announcing the termination of the war."

"Finally," Hiyakawa sighed.

Kido did not share the relief. "That will not be enough."

"Then what is His Majesty going to do?"

"He decided to be the true *Voice of the Crane*. He is going before a microphone and reading the rescript to his people."

Hiyakawa's eyebrows rose. "But that has never been done by any Emperor."

Kido nodded his agreement. "He is going to record the rescript tonight, and I want you present."

"Hai. I understand."

Kido and other aides to the Emperor immediately commenced making arrangements for the Imperial broadcast with the stunned directors of the Japan Broadcasting Corporation—the NHK.

Hiyakawa watched as the recording team arrived at the Palace complex to capture Hirohito's historic announcement. As the preparations unfolded before them, both Kido and Hiyakawa felt uneasy. There were far more soldiers than usual upon the palace grounds.

"I am afraid of what may be happening with the Imperial Guards Division," Kido said, referring to the elite soldiers who guarded the Emperor and the Palace. "Keep your wits about you."

As Hiyakawa and Kido observed the Cabinet haggling over the exact wording of the rescript, Hiyakawa received a message from a Palace guard. He read the communication twice, checked his watch and waited patiently alongside Kido.

An hour before midnight, Hirohito was driven the short distance across the Palace grounds from his living quarters to the blacked-out building of the Household Ministry.

When the Emperor entered the audience hall, they and the NHK technicians bowed to the Emperor.

Hiyakawa could not help but notice the unease of the Emperor. Hirohito stepped before the microphone and asked, "How loudly should I speak?"

An engineer respectfully suggested that the Emperor speak in his normal voice.

Hirohito took a long, deep breath before delivering a speech that Hiyakawa, Kido, and technicians in the room could hardly believe.

The Emperor was surrendering Japan.

When Hirohito completed his final word, he turned to those before and asked, "Was it all right?"

The chief engineer stammered, "There were no technical errors, but—a few words were not entirely clear."

So the Emperor, with tears stinging his eyes, read the rescript once again.

The reading was only four and a half minutes long, but the speech spanned two vinyl records. The technicians picked the first set of records for the broadcast, securing them in metal cases and then into khaki bags before presenting them to Kido.

Kido handed the historic recordings to Hiyakawa. "Put these in a safe place. A *very* safe place."

Hiyakawa accepted the precious recordings and solemnly nodded. He left the room and placed the records in a safe in a small office used by a member of the Empress's retinue—a room typically off-limits to men. His duty performed, he left to keep his appointment.

Sense of a Coup

Nakamura returned from the Palace and told us he sent a message to Hiyakawa while he waited at the gates of the Palace. A quarter hour later, he received the reply we hoped for. Hiyakawa agreed to meet with us.

We thanked Tomika for his hospitality and prepared to leave for the Palace immediately when Nakamura pulled Suki aside. "You have to stay here, Suki. I'm sorry. It may be dangerous."

Suki protested adamantly, but ultimately submitted to Nakamura's request.

Connor kissed Suki on the cheek and promised to return to her soon. The three of us promptly left for the Palace.

Instructions had been left at the guard gate to escort us directly to Hiyakawa's office. We followed the palace guards over the Nijubashi Bridge that stretched over the moat in the outer gardens and into the inner grounds of the Palace.

I had never been in the inner grounds of the Imperial Palace before—precious few Japanese citizens had—and found myself astonished by its lavish beauty. Connor and I stood in awe of what we witnessed. Yes, if this were the seat of the world as the throne maintained, I would agree at its sheer magnificence.

Within the Imperial Palace East Garden stood a stone wall that had been in place since the time when the Imperial Palace was known as Edo Castle, a structure where Samurai warriors lived from the 17th to 19th centuries.

Several minutes later, we were ushered into Hiyakawa's office where the man awaited us.

"Nakamura-san," Hiyakawa said enthusiastically. "I'm so happy and honored to meet you. And Connor and Koga, these feelings are the same for you both." He then bowed his head to Connor. "I'm sorry for the loss of your father. And your mother?"

"She died in Hiroshima."

"I am very sorry. But if it's any consolation, this terrible war will finally come to an end." He turned his attention back to Nakamura. "And what brings you here with such urgency?"

"We fear that the war may *not* end," he replied. "We have good reason to believe that there will be coup to overthrow the Emperor. Soon. If not tonight."

Hiyakawa stood speechless for a moment, staring at each of us with an expression of great distress. "How?"

Nakamura went on to explain the reasons for our visit. Suki's heated argument with Takahashi, my experience with him as well, and the sheer number of Kwantung Army troops throughout the city.

"I see," Hiyakawa replied. "I should inform you that the Emperor has recorded a surrender speech to the people. He will speak to the nation directly."

Before Nakamura could respond, the sharp report of gunfire began to echo throughout the Palace grounds.

Traitors

"It's time," Sato confided to Takahashi. "The Palace Guards are being informed that the Emperor has been duped by cowardly civilians in the Cabinet. And for that very reason, the Emperor is being removed so the county can be protected." Sato paused for a moment. "The war *will* go on."

"Hai," Takahashi replied. "What are my orders?"

"Come with me."

The two traitorous officers marched toward several soldiers with bayonets affixed to their rifles. The soldiers stopped them monetarily, but when they recognized Sato, the two men were immediately passed through. Moments later, they approached Major Hidemasa Koga, staff officer with the Imperial Guard.

"Put these around your chests," Koga ordered as he handed them white bands of material. "These will identify you from guards loyal to the Emperor."

As the two traitors draped the cloth over their jackets, Koga gave Sato a serious look. "Major Hatananka has killed Lieutenant General Takeshi Mori, commander of the Imperial Guards Division in order to prevent him from ordering the Palace Guards to stand down."

This news even shocked Sato.

"I know what you are thinking, but don't concern yourself. I've affixed Mori's seal to a false order directing the Imperial Guards to occupy the palace and its grounds, sever communications with the Palace except through Division Headquarters, occupy NHK, and prohibit all future broadcasts." He nodded his head with great satisfaction. "There will be no help coming for the Emperor."

Koga directed his attention to Takahashi. "You report to Major Kenji Hatanaka. Join his men in finding the surrender recording the Emperor had made. It must be destroyed."

"Hai," Takahashi snapped.

"Colonel Sato, you are to come with me," Koga instructed.

Sato and Koga made their way through the Palace grounds to War Minister Korechika Anami's office.

"What is happening?" demanded Anami as soon as the two men burst into the room. "What are those gunshots? And why are you here?"

"We're assuming control over the Palace in order to protect the Emperor," Koga bluntly replied, folding the lie like a well-pressed handkerchief. "And we want you to join us. To save the nation. To save Japan."

From behind his desk, the War Minister looked at both Sato and Koga with saddened, resigned eyes. "There is nothing I can do to save Japan and many a thing I *should* have done."

To Sato's surprise, Animi quickly stood up, walked over to a straw mat on the floor in front of his desk and knelt down. He pulled a dagger from his blouse and whispered, "I, with my death, humbly apologize to the Emperor for the great crimes we have committed."

His body tensed a moment before he plunged the short dagger into his stomach and across his waist, blood pumping out profusely without so much as a groan of pain.

Koga, with an unflinching, stoic expression, walked over to the bleeding man and removed the knife dangling from his torso. "Your greatest crime is cowardice." Koga then thrust the blade into Animi's neck and pushed the knife deeper until Anami's life ebbed away.

For the Sake of the Nation

"They'll be searching for the recording," Hiyakawa stated. "They must not find it, no matter the cost."

"Where is it?" Nakamura asked.

"In a small office used by a member of the Empress's retinue."

"They'll turn over every room in the Palace," Nakamura remarked. "We need to hide it in a safer place."

Hiyakawa thought on the matter for a moment. "There's a large chamber underneath the Imperial Palace. A bank vault. We can hide it there."

"Good," Nakamura said. "For the sake of the nation, let's go get those recordings."

The Hunt

The rebels, led by Major Hatanaka, spent the next several hours fruitlessly searching for the Emperor's recordings of surrender. The search was made more difficult by the normal blackouts in response to Allied bombings and by the very nature of the archaic layout of the Imperial House Ministry.

"Everyone," Hatanaka ordered of his men as his frustration mounted. "Separate and search every single room of the Palace. Leave nothing unturned." He then turned to a group of rebels. "Find the Lord Keeper of the Privy Seal, Kōichi Kido. He will know the location of the recording."

As the group of rebels split up and fanned out across the Palace, Takahashi decided to search the lower levels of the Ministry himself.

At the bottom of a stairwell, in the dim moonlight streaming in from a small decorative skylight above, Takahashi noticed a small man scurry across his path up the stairs. "Stop!" he ordered and rushed to intercept him. Upon reaching the stranger, Takahashi slammed the man against the stone wall.

"Who are you?" Takahashi hissed.

The little, bespectacled man, frightened and visibly shaken, stammered a response. "I-I... am chamberlain Yoshihiro Tokugawa."

Takahashi drew his Samurai sword and pressed the blade to the chamberlain's throat. "Tell me where the recording is hidden. Tell me or I'll split you open."

"I don't know!" the chamberlain whimpered. "I don't know where it's been hidden."

"Perhaps you should ask me," a deep, challenging voice responded from the shadows.

Takahashi turned to see Nakamura clutching the Hunjo Masamune in his hands. "Ask *me*," Nakamura reiterated.

Takahashi sneered, tossed the little chamberlain aside, and assumed the Samurai stance. "I don't know who you are, but you have only arrived in time for your death."

From behind the men, Connor stumbled upon the scene.

Before Connor could react, a rebel soldier opened a stairwell door and appeared directly in front of him. The rebel soldier quickly appraised the situation and raised his rifle toward Nakamura.

Connor reacted instinctively and without hesitation. He leapt upon the soldier and wrestled the man to the ground.

Distracted by the altercation, Nakamura did not see Takahashi leap forward, raise his sword, and bring it down with great force, the blade effortlessly sliced a piece of flesh from Nakamura's upper arm.

Nakamura staggered forward, but managed to raise his sword and attack his foe.

While the two men clashed, and the piercing sound of metal against metal filled the stone corridor, Connor and the rebel soldier rolled down the stairwell towards the two dueling Samurai.

In what seemed an eternity, the four bodies intertwined as one in the semi-dark space. Primitive grunts and curses filled the stairwell until a shot rang out.

Both the rebel soldier and Connor backed off only to see Takahashi staring down at his bloody Samurai sword. But he was not gawking at his sword. He stared in shock at the gaping bullet hole ripped through his chest by the errant discharge of the guard wrestling with Connor.

Takahashi's eyes rolled back momentarily, and he collapsed down the stairwell. His heart stopped beating.

The rebel soldier regained his senses, shoved Connor into a darkened corner, and aimed the tip of his rifle at the boy.

Connor whispered a small prayer, closed his eyes, and waited for the inevitable.

A spray of warm, salty liquid suddenly splattered across his face. He opened his eyes, noticed the blood that coated his skin, and watched as the rebel soldier, nearly cut in two, drop at his feet.

Nakamura stood over the severed soldier with the Hunjo Masamune clutched in his fists.

Connor saw the wound leaking blood down Nakamura's arm. "That looks really bad."

"Hai, but I'll survive," Nakamura groaned.

"Now. Where are the recordings?" asked a familiar voice from behind them.

Connor and Nakamura spun around to see Sato holding his service pistol leveled at them both.

"Go to hell," Nakamura snarled.

"I most probably will," he replied, and without hesitation, shot Nakamura pointblank in the chest.

"No!" Connor cried as he ran to Nakamura side.

"Now tell me, ijin," Sato growled, "Where are the recordings?"

Connor glared up at Sato, his eyes burning into the man who now represented every injustice and betrayal he had received in his entire life.

Sato laughed at the boy's expression, causing the scar on his face to look more hideous than ever. "You will take me to the recordings—or do you pretend to be a hero of Japan?" Saying this aloud made him laugh. "A hero of Japan. An American. The Emperor's savior!"

In the dim light, Connor slowly stood, quietly picked up the Hunjo Masamune lying next to Nakamura, and hid it to his side in the dim light. "Hai," he replied. "I will take you to the recordings. Follow me."

Satisfied, Sato lowered his gun slightly to follow the American.

Connor took one step forward, then pivoted his body and swung the Samurai sword with all the force he could muster.

Connor's unexpected move caught Sato by surprise, and the blade of the sword found its mark. The blade sliced Sato across the hip, and he collapsed to the ground, dropping his service pistol and howling in agony.

Connor picked up Sato's pistol and thrust the barrel into the man's forehead. "You destroyed my people, and for that, you have to pay."

Sato's expression hardened. "So, you will kill in the name of justice?"

Connor's answer was to cock the gun.

But Sato, sitting in his blood on the cold ground of the stairwell, calmly rose to his knees, reached inside his tunic and withdrew out a small sword—a tantō.

Connor began to squeeze the trigger when Nakamura shouted from the corner of the stairwell, "No!"

Connor gazed at Nakamura, relieved that he was still alive. "But why? He deserves death."

"Hai. That he does, but leave him to his honor," Nakamura said as he limped forward and placed a bloody hand on Connor's shoulder.

With his pistol still trained on Sato, Connor watched the traitor thrust the tantō into his abdomen, then pulled the small sword from right to left until his intestines spilled out onto the floor.

Nakamura held out his hand to Connor, and the boy instinctively reacted, handing the Hunjo Masamune to the warrior monk. Nakamura raised the blade high over his head, and in one smooth gesture, decapitated Sato.

The two stood quietly for a moment until Nakamura stated coldly, "Let's go to Hiyakawa."

By Order of General Tanaka

Soon after their arrival at the door to the vault room, six rebel soldiers approached.

"Drop your weapons," ordered a rebel sergeant.

Both men conceded. Connor dropped his pistol and Nakamura placed his sword on the ground.

"Open up the room," the sergeant ordered.

"We can't," Nakamura simply replied.

The sergeant sneered at Nakamura's response and silently ordered his men to raise their rifles.

Suddenly a voice barked down the hall. "Stand down," was the command from a rebel Captain accompanied by a dozen rebel troops. The Captain walked up to the sergeant. "We are surrendering the Palace. Commander of the Eastern Region, General Tanaka, has ordered us to leave and return to our barracks."

There was some reluctance from the sergeant when the Captain barked, "That's an order."

The Captain marched off, leading the rebels out of the basement.

Hiyakawa opened the vault door from inside. "Is it over?" he asked.

"Hai. It's over," Nakamura replied.

To Suffer the Insufferable

We took Nakamura to the clinic at the Palace for medial care, then we returned the next morning to the restaurant where Suki anxiously awaited.

She and the other patrons in the restaurant were listening to the radio in stunned awe.

The Emperor was speaking.

It was shocking enough to hear the Emperor's decree, but even more unexpected, he uttered the decree *himself.* It was the first time any regular Japanese citizen had ever heard the Emperor's voice.

Suki gazed at Nakamura with confusion muddling her eyes.

"To endure the unendurable and suffer what is not sufferable," Connor stated. "Does that mean Japan has finally surrendered?"

"Hai," Nakamura replied. "That's exactly what it means." He gazed through the restaurant window and peered out over the ruins of Tokyo.

"What do we do now?" Suki asked.

Nakamura turned from the window and walked over to Connor and Suki. "We rebuild." He placed his hands on their shoulders. "Take the best of the past and build towards the future. That's your responsibility now."

Suki nodded towards Connor. "The best of the past," she acknowledged.

"And the best of the future," Connor added smiling at her.

Nakamura looked at me. "And what about you Koga? What path do you take?"

I smiled. "Simple. I'm going to write a report on the events of last night. And win a Nobel Prize, of course!"

Epilogue

But, alas, that was not to be.

News of the *incident*—that's the name they called the event—was shelved. A war weary public was not to know that there was a bold and very public attempt upon the throne.

During the Allied occupation, the incident was revealed to General Douglas MacArthur, Supreme Commander of the Allied Powers, as proof that the Emperor wanted to surrender Japan and to spare Hirohito from the hangman's noose.

It wasn't until decades later that the truth of the Kyūjō incident would finally be made public. But by that time, I was back in the United States with my family, living the American life I always dreamed of experiencing.

Connor remained in Japan and eventually became an interpreter for the Allied occupation and lived the Japanese life he always wanted...

...with honor.

Major Historical Characters
Mentioned In The Book

Emperor Hirohito—Emperor of Japan. A peaceful man. However, he is no politician.

Vice-Admiral Yamamoto—a leading advocate of peace and reason in the Imperial Navy. He was the mastermind behind the attack on Pearl Harbor.

Princes Mikasa, Higashikuni and Takamatsu—member of the royal family who are against going to war and are trying to shield the Emperor from the militarists.

Prince Chichibu—Emperor Hirohito's brother, has repeatedly counseled the Emperor to implement direct imperial rule, even if that means suspending the constitution and creating a military dictatorship.

John Rabe—Director of the German Siemens AG China Corporation.

Minoru Genda—a staunch believer in naval air power. Helped plan the attack on Pearl Harbor.

Fumimaro Konoe—Prime Minister.

General Tomoyuki Yamashita—commander of the crack Twenty-Fifth Army invasion force. His men called him the *Tiger of Malaya*.

Liwayway—Female Filipino guerrilla leader who dresses up to show the troops that she is fearless and calm, not afraid to die in combat. She combines her femininity with ferociousness and that earns their respect.

Major Fictional Characters
Mentioned In The Book

Yoshihara Koga—A Japanese-American reporter is introduced on page one to tell the story about Connor.

Connor Williams—An American teenager is an innocent soul coming of age against the backdrop of an ill-conceived war. Soon to lead a flight of kamikaze planes against the U.S. Fleet of Okinawa.

Akihito Fujiyama—A Commander and fighter pilot in the Imperial Japanese Navy. Fujiyama acts as military attaché to the U.S. Navy. He lives with his wife, Miyoko, and their sons. Hiryo is fourteen and Yoshi is thirteen.

Kenta Hiyakawa—A Foreign Office diplomat. He is a thorn in the side of the militarists. He is a distant cousin of the Emperor, thus a confirmation of the rumors that he has the Emperor's ear.

Barbara Hiyakawa—Wife of Hiyakawa, a tall, elegant Caucasian American woman with short auburn hair. She is bold and outspoken.

Miyoko Fujiyama—A gentle and loving woman, wife to Fujiyama.

Tomoko Sakura—Yoshihara's editor, who sees himself as an ethical Samurai for truth, like his hero, Edward G. Robinson.

Haru Sato—A Kempeitai colonel on the Supreme Military Council that sits in Army/Navy Imperial Headquarters. Part of the military police arm and leads the Yakuza.

Captain Hidaka Takahashi—A brutal Japanese officer in love with Sui, Fujiyama's daughter. An aide de camp to Colonel Sato.

Kenji—Youngest Fujiyama son enamored with American culture.

Suki—Fujiyama's only daughter, a young girl, just shy of 5 feet, with long, black hair that hangs over dark eyes that dance on high cheekbones. Connor is enamored with her.

Mai—Miyoko's sister. She has been watching over Suki and Kenji while Fujiyama was on assignment in America.

Father Marquette—A priest who runs the French *Catholic mission* in *Manchuria* for the Société des Missions Étrangères de Paris.

Huan Quang—A villager

Masao Koga—Yoshihara's older brother whom Koga thought was dead. He succumbed to the propaganda and joined the Black Ocean Society, an ultra-nationalist organization.

Kodo Tento, Goro Yoshida and Jiro Miyagi—Members of the Yakuza. Connor attracted to Kodo, the tattooed girl. Led by Sato who is also part of the Kempeitei.

Black Patch—A close school friend of Kenji's. He is called Black Patch because of the dark brown birthmark that covers almost a quarter of his face.

Williams—Connor's cruel American father.

Aiko—Niece to Miyako, daughter of Mai. She is a geisha and Connor will fall in love with her.

Nakamura—He is a warrior monk with an unusual Samurai past.

Matsumuro—wealthy sponsor of Aiko.

Lieutenant Wantanabi—A squad leader on Saipan.

About the Author

Frank F. Fiore is a five-star rated author of novels in multiple genres including Contemporary Fiction, Tecno-Thrillers, Action/Adventures, Sci-Fi, Historical Fiction, and Westerns. He lives in Arizona with his fetching wife, Lynne.

Connect with Frank online at:

www.frankfiore.com

Also Available From

WordCrafts Press

In Times Like These
Gail Kittleson

Angela's Treasures
Marian Rizzo

The Pruning
Jan Cline

The Restless Earth
Alan Cockrell

Oh, to Grace
Abby Rosser

www.wordcrafts.net